Proposal For Love

Sharon C. Cooper

ISBN: 978-1-946172-01-3
Paperback

Formatted by Enterprise Book Services, LLC

Disclaimer
This story is a work of fiction. Names, characters, and incidents are either products of the author's imagination or are used fictitiously. Any resemblance to actual events, locales, organizations or persons, living or dead, is entirely coincidental.

Acknowledgements

Special thanks to my amazing husband, Al, who I absolutely adore! Thank you for putting up with my long writing hours and for helping me with "research". *wink, wink*

To my awesome critique partners – you know who you are. I can't imagine this writing journey without all of you! Love you guys!

To my beta reader (B.S.) - You ROCK! Love you to pieces!

To my readers – It's because of you I do this writing thing! Thank you for your continued support, hilarious emails, and for spreading the word about my books! I so appreciate and love you all!

Much love,
Sharon

Chapter One

You can do this. Just relax.

Liberty Stewart stood in front of the mirror in her bathroom, the size of a Cracker Jack box, struggling to calm her shaky hands long enough to apply lipstick. As the time grew closer to start the first project at her new job, the more nervous she became. No amount of self-talk helped. One disappointment after another could do that to a person.

Liberty's hand slipped, spreading red lipstick past her lips. "Dammit. Why even bother?" She slammed the tube down on the vanity not caring that part of the brand-new lipstick broke off into the sink. She hated wearing the crap anyway.

Wiping the red smear from her face only made things worse. She threw the washcloth into the sink and rested her palms on the vanity. "Relax and pull yourself together."

Dropping her chin to her chest, she sucked in a long, deep breath before releasing it slowly. Finally landing a position with a reputable company should be all the encouragement she needed to prove her life was on the right track. Yet, her self-esteem had taken so many hits over the last few years, she worried she'd never get her life straightened out. Searching for work in Chicago for over eight months with one door after another being slammed in her face kept replaying in her mind.

What if this new job didn't work out? What if she ended up on the streets again? What if she was being set up for another let down?

No. No negative talk. You can do this.

When she finally glanced up at the mirror again, her sister stood in the bathroom doorway, hands on her hips.

"Really, Liberty?"

"What?" She picked up the tube of lipstick and replaced the cap before wiping out the sink.

"You've been in here for thirty minutes touching up your makeup and you look the same as you did when you first walked in here. What the heck? Why are you so nervous about this assignment?"

"Maybe because this is the first *real* job I've had in a while. Or maybe because this is the first time in a long time I'm in charge of a project of this magnitude. A sixty-million-dollar project, I might add. Or maybe it's because the future of my job is dependent upon the success of said project." Liberty shrugged. "I don't know, Demi. Pick one. Heck, it's not even just about the job. It's my life in general. I can't afford to screw this up." Her new boss had made it very clear that Liberty's future with the company depended on the success of this assignment.

"Sis, you got this." Demi placed a hand on her shoulder and squeezed. "Look at you. You're beautiful, intelligent and the most amazing, bravest woman I know."

Liberty stared at her reflection only seeing a thirty-four-year-old broken woman hiding behind a made-up face, classy new haircut, and a pink blouse that highlighted her chestnut skin tone. She looked professional on the outside, but a roaring tornado best described her inner turmoil.

"You've been through hell," Demi continued. "Yet, here you are starting over in a new city, and finally have a job that can get you on your feet. No matter what that asshole ex-husband of yours did, you didn't let him win. You haven't given up."

Liberty didn't want to tell her sister that she had given up more times than not. She couldn't count how many mistakes she'd made or how trusting the wrong person had ruined her. Trying to pull her life together was proving harder than she ever imagined, and if it weren't for her sister, Liberty didn't know where she'd be. Demi had convinced her to move to Cincinnati to be closer to her.

Liberty's gaze took in her sister. Demi Jackson, three years younger, was one of the most pulled together women Liberty knew. Tall, with straightened hair hanging past her shoulders, and makeup applied to perfection, she was beautiful by anyone's standards. As a successful event planner, owning her own business at the age of thirty-one, and engaged to a doctor, Demi had done well for herself.

"I'm so proud of you," Liberty said.

Demi hugged her from behind, her head resting on Liberty's shoulder as they stared at each other in the mirror. "And I'm proud of you. I know I've said it before, but thank you for everything you did for me. If it weren't for your sacrifices, I wouldn't be where I am today. I just wish you would've been honest with me years ago. Together we could have prevented some of the crap you went through."

"Maybe, but I did what I needed to do at the time." Liberty turned and wrapped her arms around her sister's shoulders. "Our family has been through so much. Even though Mom and Dad aren't with us anymore, I'm glad you and I are in the same city now. I have missed you so much."

"And I've missed you. Whatever happened in the past is in the past. It's time we move forward," Demi said. They held each other for a moment longer before stepping apart. "I have to go, but I have no doubt you're going to rock this new project!"

"God, I hope you're right."

*

"They need us more than we need them. Maybe we should think about submitting the proposal on our own," Nathaniel Jenkins-Moore said as he and his twin brother strolled through the back door of Jenkins & Sons Construction. The smell of fresh paint from the recently remodeled first floor conference rooms greeted them before they reached the stairs.

His brother, Nick, shook his head and slowed. "Not that I don't think we'd have a shot, but LCA Construction is four times larger than us. Partnering with them will give us the perfect opportunity to get our names out there even more."

Nate and Nick took turns pleading their case as they headed up the stairs not stopping until they reached Nate's office.

"Come on, man. I have a good feeling about all of this." Nick dropped down in the guest chair in front of the desk. "And do I need to remind you that the Unity Tower building is a sixty-million-dollar project?"

"I know, but if we go for the job ourselves, we won't have to settle for forty percent of that. We can keep a hundred percent of the net profits."

Nate faced his computer screen and scrolled through his emails. Tired of listening to his brother go on and on about the project, he was tempted to concede to the idea just to shut him up.

"Nate, I don't want to let this opportunity pass us by. Besides, the person overseeing the proposal will be here in a couple of hours to meet with you. We can't back out now."

Nate rocked in his seat and stared at his brother. Nick was right about one thing. Partnering with LCA might be a once in a lifetime opportunity. Since J&S was the largest minority-owned construction company in the area, Nate guessed that was why the invitation to partner came their way. Submitting a proposal with a large minority company would make LCA eligible for federal funding.

"All right. We'll do this, but if I fall behind in my work, you're picking up the slack."

Nick frowned. "Why would you get behind?"

"Because LCA has to go through our books, get a feel for our business practices, and who knows what else. They have to know that we run a viable business before they include us in this propo—"

"Nate, I fall more and more in love with you every day."

Nate glanced at his office door where their receptionist, Tammy, stood in the doorway a huge smile on her face and holding a crystal vase of red roses. Nate could smell the potent fragrance of the flowers from across the office.

"These are so beautiful."

Nate returned her smile. "Who said those were from me?"

"Because you and Grandpa Jenkins are the only thoughtful men around here." She looked pointedly at Nick. Tammy worked for the company the past ten years. That loyalty qualified her as an honorary family member.

Nick frowned. "If you're trying to insult me on a sly, it's not working. I'm a happily married man. I can't go around buying flowers for other women. Sumeera would kill me," he said of his wife of six months.

"Yeah, whatever." Tammy rolled her eyes good-naturedly and returned her attention to Nate. "Thank you. This was very thoughtful."

Nate stood and strolled across the office and kissed her cheek. "My pleasure, and happy birthday. *We* all just wanted you to know how special you are to us."

Nate closed the door behind her.

"See that's the shit that's going to get us slapped with some type of sexual discrimination lawsuit. She's going to fall for your charming ass only to realize you do that crap for every woman you know."

Nate waved him off. His brother and cousins had dubbed him a modern-day Prince Charming. According to them, he rescued every damsel in distress and they fell in love with him without much effort on his part.

"I don't do that for every woman I know. Besides, there's no harm in showing a little appreciation for hard work. No one has screamed sexual harassment or anything else like that in all the years we've been in business. I doubt it'll happen just because I buy the support staff flowers on their birthday."

"All right, but you're on your own if your good deeds come back to bite you in the ass."

"I'll keep that in mind. Now, if I have to spend a chunk of the next coming weeks working with LCA's project manager, then you and Toni are going to have to pick up the slack around here."

Their cousin, Toni Jenkins-Logan, was a plumber by trade but helped out in the office whenever he or Nick took vacation.

"Fine. Whatever it takes. And while you're working on that grant proposal, add some dollars for additional clerical staff. Assuming we beat out everyone else, we'll definitely need more help around here." Nick stretched his arms high over his head and yawned.

"Man, that's the third time you've yawned in the last five minutes. What's up with you?"

"Two words. Chanelle Moore."

Nate smiled at the mention of his niece. Nick's wife, Sumeera, had given birth almost two months ago and Nate was already attached to the little cutie. When his brother asked him to be her godfather the day she was born, the request surprised Nate, but he planned to take his role seriously. He loved kids and though he didn't have any of his own yet, he was already crazy in love with that baby girl.

"I can't imagine that little cutie-pie is giving you any trouble."

"Ha! Spend the night tonight, and when she cries—every two hours—you can see to her needs. Meera and I could use a few uninterrupted hours of sleep."

"Sorry, no can do. I have dinner plans tonight. Maybe another time," Nate said unapologetically.

"Yeah, I thought so." Nick stood. "You date more than I ever did. I can't understand why you haven't settled down yet. Between the two of us, you were the one most likely to get married first."

In all of the women he'd dated, there had only been one he'd ever considered proposing to, and that was in his last year of college. Since then, he hadn't been willing to give his heart to another only to have it stomped on.

"Who you going out with tonight?"

"A woman I met at a networking event two weeks ago." After talking with her on the phone a few times, he suggested they meet for drinks. Now Nate was having second thoughts. She was beautiful, smart, and they had enough in common, but casual dating had lost its appeal. He was struggling with that realization because after college, he didn't let women get too close. But lately, he'd been thinking about what his brother and so many other men he knew had—a wife and kids to go home to.

"Well, have fun. I'm out of here. I'll be on a job site for most of the afternoon, but let me know how the meeting goes."

"Will do."

*

Hours later, Nate headed to the first floor to meet LCA's project manager. Reservations about the proposal process plagued him. Even with signed non-disclosure forms from both companies, he was hesitant to share pricing plans, profit models, or much of any information with LCA.

Tammy glanced up from her computer when he approached the front desk. "Thanks again for the flowers. You definitely made my day."

"My pleasure. I'm glad you like them."

Nate knew she loved roses. Buying her flowers to celebrate her birthday had been a simple gesture, and a way to let her know they appreciated her commitment to the company.

"Which conference room is Miss Stewart in?"

"I put her in C. Let me know if you two need anything."

"I will, thanks," Nate said over his shoulder as he headed down the hall. A satisfied smile lifted the corners of his mouth as he surveyed the new photos of construction sites gracing the wall. They were almost finished with the second phase of the four-part renovation of the building, and Nate was pleased with how everything was turning out. The new look was a great advertisement of their workers' skills.

Nate's dress shoes clicked against the shiny travertine floors as he passed several glass enclosed conference rooms. At first, he didn't think the transparent walls and doors were a good idea, but with the fabric blinds hanging at all the windows, meetings could become private in an instant.

Nate slowed when he approached conference room C where a woman stood at the window, her back to the door. He rotated his shoulders a few times and shook off a shudder as a sense of deja vu settled around him. He wasn't sure what caused the odd sensation as he drank in the woman's stature.

From the short distance, she appeared tall at around 5'8" wearing a pink blouse tucked into a straight black skirt. His body stirred at how well the garment hugged her perfectly round butt. No doubt she was a runner if her shapely calves were any indication. The black high heels added emphasis to her toned legs. Hair cut into a short, stylish bob that was long on one side hid her profile, but what he did see piqued his interest.

Nate pushed open the door and strolled in.

"Ms. Stewart, sorry to keep you waiting. I'm Na..." The words lodged in his throat and heat soared through his body when the woman turned to face him.

"Nate," she said on a gasp, her mouth hanging open.

He shook his head and blinked several times to ensure he wasn't seeing things. Tension seized his body. Shock shifted to disbelief which quickly turned to anger.

"Kayla." Disgust dripped from the single word. Rage crawled over his body like a trail of army ants, irking him more than her presence. "Whatever you're selling, I'm not buying. Get out!"

Chapter Two

Liberty jerked as if she'd been slapped, shaken by his words. Unease crept up her spine at the lethalness in his stare, only enhancing the anxiety she had walked into the building with. She couldn't get her mouth to work. Rooted in place she wasn't sure what to say or do. And he had called her Kayla. A name from her distant past. A name that no longer represented her. A name she hadn't heard in a long time…especially from his mouth.

Okay, Liberty. Get it together. You're here to do a job. Nothing else.

Despite the hostility radiating off of Nate, she wasn't sure how long she stood staring at the god-like Adonis. Dark-chocolate with baby smooth skin, a perfectly trimmed goatee, and smoky-brown eyes so intense they could drill a hole right through her.

Liberty swallowed as her gaze traveled the length of him. Even with his body sheathed in a light-gray polo shirt and dress slacks, she could tell that he had bulked up in all the right places since she'd last seen him.

Her gaze returned to his eyes and the storm brewing within caused her to tremble. A whirlwind of emotions twisted inside her and she moved closer to the chair that held her laptop bag. She'd often wondered what would happen if they ever ran into each other again. Now she knew.

Attraction, lust, need and a bit of fear had her nerves on edge. It didn't help that the energy he'd brought into the room could ignite a wildfire. Why did their first meeting in thirteen years have to be now? She had only been in town for a few weeks and at the new job less than that. The last thing she needed was to run into the only man who'd ever meant anything to her. The only man she had ever loved...and left.

When she noted the first name of the Jenkins & Sons contact person, brief memories of Nate and their time together flitted across her mind. Never in a million years had she expected to see *her* Nate.

God, please don't let him be the Nathaniel that I'm supposed to meet with.

"I'm here to meet with Nathaniel Jenkins," Liberty finally said.

"Why?" Nate's voice boomed over the light jazz playing in the overhead speakers.

The room closed in around her, and she took a step backward only to bump into the window she stood at earlier.

"Are you hard of hearing, Kayla? I asked why. What do you want?"

She shook her head. "It's Liberty," she said barely above a whisper before clearing her throat, willing herself to speak up. "My name is Liberty."

Nate let out a ruthless laugh. "Still playing games, huh."

"It's no game, Nate. I no longer go by Kayla. I haven't in a long time, and I'm here to meet with Nathaniel Jenkins regarding the Unity Tower proposal with LCA."

God, please don't let...

"Nathaniel Jenkins-Moore. My full name. My family owns Jenkins & Sons."

Liberty felt as if someone had punched her in the gut. She couldn't catch a break. Her life continued to throw one catastrophe after another, but this...this was too much.

Nate had gone by Moore in college. How had she not known he had two last names?

Because you did more kissing and hugging than talking, her brain taunted.

Nate didn't take his dark gaze off of her. In college, there had always been a strong, powerful presence about him, but never scary or intimidating like now.

As he approached her, the warmth spreading through her body had nothing to do with the heat outside. It also had nothing to do with the long-sleeved blouse she was wearing. No, what she was feeling had everything to do with how Nate still had a powerful effect on her whenever he was near. Her body vibrated with an electric sizzle that only he could rouse.

Liberty swallowed hard. "Um, I—I'm shocked to see you. Why did you go by Moore instead of Jenkins in college?"

He shook his head. "Doesn't matter, *Kayla* Jackson. I'm not sure what type of game you're playing by being here, but—"

"I don't play games. My—"

"Don't you?" he fumed, his tone menacing as he moved closer, less than twelve inches between them. She stood her ground, her body unable to move from the intensity of his stare. "I seem to remember you being very good at stringing me along, making me fall for you, and then opting for the better prize."

"Nate."

"Oh wait." He snapped his fingers. "It wasn't quite like that. I think your exact words were, *I love you, Nate, but I have to think of my future.* I guess I wasn't good enough for your bougie ass, huh?"

Defeat rested in Liberty's chest as she listened to him recall one of the biggest mistakes she'd ever made. "Nate, that was a long time ago. I'm not that person anymore."

"Aren't you?"

"No, I'm not. I'm here to do a job. That's it. I don't want any trouble, and I'm not here to cause you any trouble." Getting her nerves under control, she was determined to do the job she'd been hired to do. She pulled her computer from the laptop bag.

"Stop right there." Liberty startled when Nate placed a hand over hers, a zing of electricity shooting up her arm. He removed his hand just as quick, clearly feeling the same shock wave. "You're not staying," he snapped.

"I understand that we have a history, Nate, but this is my job," she said, still recovering from his touch. "This has nothing to do with our past."

"This has *everything* to do with our past! I don't trust you, Kayla! My experience with you has taught me a few things. Never take anyone at their word alone. Never give your heart unless you know it's in good hands. And never trust a pretty face because you're bound to get stabbed in the chest."

"Please don't do this."

"Get. Out!"

"I'm not that person anymore, Nate."

"Oh yeah, that's right. You've changed your name. Just because you go by a different name and changed your appearance," he said waving his hand up and down the length of her, "doesn't mean your soul is different."

Liberty stood transfixed, trying to find the words to save this project. To save her job.

"I said, get out!" he yelled, his eyes hard and unyielding, his body rigid with tension.

Liberty hurried and put her laptop into the bag. When she went to pass Nate, she wanted to try one last time to convince him to work with her.

He took a huge step back. "Get the hell out of here before I have you thrown out!"

Instead of saying anything else, she rushed to the door, pissed at the dark cloud that seemed to still be following her around.

I've got to fix this. I can't lose this job.

*

Liberty paced past her sister's kitchen table and halted at the edge of the family room before turning and retracing her steps. She wasn't sure how many paths she'd made since showing up at the house, but if she kept it up she was sure to wear out the floor.

"Can you please sit down and eat? As skinny as you've gotten, you can't afford to go without a meal."

"I'm not hungry," Liberty said to her sister, unable to stop moving. Nate's reaction and hurtful words were at the forefront of her mind.

"Demi, I have never seen him that angry before. He didn't even seem like the same person."

When Liberty had walked away from him in college, Nate had been more confused than angry. Then again, it's not like she stuck around after breaking up with him. She didn't even want to think about how angry he had probably been once the information settled in.

"You haven't seen him in like forever, not since college. I think it's safe to say you both have changed." Her sister, though younger, was always the voice of reason. Liberty had called her the moment she left Jenkins & Sons.

Liberty's stomach churned, anxiousness clawing through her body. She dropped down in one of the kitchen chairs and groaned. Considering the day had started out promising, it had quickly taken a nose dive after running into Nate. If it weren't for bad luck, she wouldn't have any luck at all.

"What am I going to do?" she asked more to herself than her sister.

Instead of the salad Liberty expected, Demi placed a large slice of chocolate cake in front of her.

"Eat, and before you ask, it's sugar free, butter free, and free of everything else that makes a chocolate cake good," Demi cracked, a wicked grin covering her lips. She often teased, telling Liberty that eating only vegetables was like eating cardboard.

Liberty stared at the delicious looking three-layer cake. She'd been a vegan for five years, only recently adding dairy and eggs occasionally into her diet. She wasn't a big sweet eater, but the dessert could tempt the most dedicated dieter.

"I thought we were having lunch. As in a big salad with carrots, tomatoes and maybe broccoli. What happened?"

"After your call, I felt you needed to start with something more decadent than the cardboard you usually eat."

Her sister always gave her a hard time about her eating regimen, but Liberty appreciated that Demi supported her vegetarian lifestyle.

Liberty's mouth watered in anticipation. "What's really in this?"

"Don't worry. It's vegan. If today is one of those days that you're not eating eggs, you're good. I picked the cake up from that place on Montgomery Road that you mentioned the other day."

Liberty's heart melted a little at the kind gesture. She ate a few bites of the cake, struggling to swallow past the lump in her throat. Thoughts of Nate and the Unity Tower project filtered into her mind again.

She pushed the cake aside and laid her head on her folded arms on top of the table.

"I can't believe this is happening. If I screw up this proposal, I'm going to be out of a job," she mumbled against her arm. "How could Nate treat me like this?"

"Don't give up yet, sis. I'm sure he was just shocked. All you have to do is call him tomorrow. He will have calmed down by then and the two of you will be able to discuss the past and present like adults."

Liberty shook her head, her hair swishing back and forth. "You didn't see him, Demi. You didn't hear him." She lifted her head. "Heck I stood there like a complete fool, shocked at not only seeing him, but at how different he seemed."

"Well, you have to admit. He probably felt as if he was seeing a ghost. Imagine how you'd feel. You guys dated exclusively for months. He even professed his love to you. And then the day he graduated from college, you dump him for someone else without warning. And that's not even the worse part. You ma—"

"Don't. Please don't say it."

Being reminded of all that she'd done was like getting punched in the gut. No matter how many times over the years she tried justifying her decisions, she still felt like the lowest form of human life.

"You hooked up with the man you said you would never give the time of day to again," her sister continued. "The man who *Nate* rescued you from. The man who—"

Liberty leaped up, practically knocking over the chair. "Stop. Please. Just stop. You're not making me feel better. I was young and dumb. I'm not that person anymore."

She'd said the same thing to Nate, and now sounded like a broken record. Liberty had to prove to him and to herself that she wasn't that same woman. And she wasn't going to let Nate or anyone else ruin this job for her. She'd been through hell the last few years. Clawed herself out of the gutter her ex-husband had dumped her into. No way would she let another man mistreat her.

"There is one thing you haven't mentioned about the infamous Nate."

Liberty sighed and accepted the tossed salad her sister handed her before they both sat at the round, glass table. She was so done discussing Nate, at least for today. At least until she figured out what to do about the Unity Tower project and his role in it.

"How did he look? When you described Nate while you were in college, you made him sound like some type of African prince. Does he look the same?"

"He's moved up from prince to Nubian god," Liberty mumbled with disdain, angry she was still attracted to him. After the way he behaved, she shouldn't feel anything for the man. Unfortunately, his nasty words that had played on a loop in her mind all the way to her sister's house hadn't lessened his appeal. Probably because deep inside, Liberty felt she deserved it a little, after what she had done to him.

"He was *hot* when we attend Northwestern, but now…"

"Well, dang. I can't wait to meet him."

Liberty's fork stopped short of her mouth. "What makes you think you'll meet him?"

Her sister shrugged while she finished chewing. "I don't know. Just a feeling."

"Well your feelings are off kilter. I don't know how yet, but Nate and I will only have a working relationship. At least I hope." At the moment, Liberty wasn't sure how she was going to get him to listen to her. Let alone work with her.

After another few bites of her salad, she set the fork down and stood. All the talk about Nate had her mind whirling with memories she thought she had sealed away.

"He's not the same man. The man I remember was charming, had an easy smile, and was a perfect gentleman. He would have never raised his voice at me…or any woman. I can't believe I did this to him. Turned him into a—a jerk."

"Really, Liberty? I know you're all that," Demi said sarcastically, "but you can't take ownership for his rudeness. If he's still holding a grudge after all these years, he's the one with the problem."

"I hurt him," Liberty choked out. "The weeks leading up to graduation we had talked about our future together. How we were going to try and make a long-distance relationship work while he lived in Ohio and I finish at Northwestern. You didn't see him the day I broke up with him. He was devastated."

"Yeah, I bet he was, but it wasn't an easy decision for you. I might've still been young, but now I understand why you did what you did."

"How…" Liberty's voice hitched as a stab of pain pierced her heart. "How am I ever going to be able to face him again?"

"I think the bigger question is—how are you going to save this project and keep your job?

"I wish I knew."

Chapter Three

Nate hung up the phone and returned his attention to the file on his desk. He'd read the same information three times and still didn't know what it said. Focusing was impossible with his thoughts constantly drifting back to his morning with Kayla.

He still couldn't believe he'd seen her. Until he had gone off on her and brought up what she'd done to him, he thought he had moved on.

"Apparently, not," he grumbled, rubbing his forehead.

What were the chances? Of all the people who could be a part of the Unity Tower project, why her? And what was up with the name change? And why did she have to look so good? Gone was the girl he had fallen in love with almost at first sight, and in her place was a stunning woman who made his heart race just recalling their encounter earlier. And those eyes. Those dark, exotic eyes and that sexy voice still had an effect on him.

"Let it go, Nate. It's done. Over." As far as he was concerned, if he never saw her again it would be too soon.

The best way to rid his mind of one woman was to call another. He reached for his cell phone, but before he could make the call his door swung open.

"What the hell have you done?" his brother roared, slamming the door closed. "Have you lost your damn mind? I thought we agreed that LCA was a go. Why am I receiving calls from the project manager saying that you kicked her out this morning? And why didn't I hear about this from you? I shouldn't be blindsided by a stranger when my own brother could have called and filled me in."

"Hello to you too, my brotha." Nate leaned in his leather desk chair and rocked slightly, waiting for his brother to calm down.

"Don't *my brotha* me! What the hell happened? When did you start saying one thing and then doing something different? We had an agreement."

"I know the representative for LCA from way back, and she can't be trusted. No way am I sharing any of Jenkins's business information with her. It's not going to happen." Thanks to Kayla Jackson, he hadn't trusted another woman outside of the women in his family since she betrayed him all those years ago. He never would again.

"Are you telling me you're letting some personal feelings get in the way of a sixty-million-dollar project?"

"I'm telling you that I can't work with the project manager. If LCA wants to send someone else, fine. I'll reconsider our company's involvement."

"Are you even hearing yourself? *You* are not Jenkins & Sons. All of us are. You don't get to make decisions like that alone."

Nate stood slowly, his anger on the brink of exploding as he glared at his brother.

"Need I remind you of a similar situation you were in a few months ago. Does the name Russell McCray ring a bell? If I'm not mistaken, you didn't bring the decision to turn down that contract to the board. You decided that working with that company wasn't in the best interest and we trusted your judgment."

"Dammit, Nate! Don't try to twist this shit. That situation involved *my wife* and was totally different and you know it."

Nate wasn't about to let his brother know that he agreed—that situation had been different. McCray, despite being Sumeera's father, was a wealthy, egotistical jerk, with mental issues according to Nick. Owner of a project development company, McCray had awarded them a contract to build one of his strip malls. During final negotiations, he started jerking them around before they knew his relationship to Sumeera. Nick almost killed the guy when he arrived home one night and found McCray manhandling Sumeera. Nate hadn't been there, but he had never known his brother to get that angry at anyone.

"Bringing Russell into this conversation was a low blow. Not only did I fear my wife's life was in danger then, but I still don't trust him now around my family."

"I know, and you're right. It was a poor comparison. I shouldn't have brought it up."

Since that altercation, Sumeera obtained a restraining order against her father. Her mother had relocated to Cincinnati after the incident, immediately cutting ties with him. That wasn't enough for Nick. He hired a private investigator, their cousin Peyton's husband, to keep tabs on Sumeera's father. McCray was still living in New York, but had visited Cincinnati a few times recently trying to win back Sumeera's mother.

"I also nixed the contract with McCray because our reputation was at stake. I couldn't trust that McCray wouldn't do something to sabotage our company."

"And I don't trust Kayla Jackson. No way am I letting her near our business." Nate returned to his seat and massaged his temples. He didn't know what he needed more right now, sleep or a stiff drink.

"Wait. Who the hell is Kayla Jackson? The woman who called me was Liberty Stewart."

Nate dropped his hands to his desk. He had never spoken of Kayla. At least not by name. Nate had met her after Christmas break his senior year at Northwestern. They'd run into each other, literally, at a restaurant he ate at all the time. And from that day they had been inseparable, except for when he spent Spring Break that year overseas.

"Well?" Nick demanded, an eyebrow raised.

"Liberty Stewart and Kayla Jackson are one and the same."

"LCA's project manager? The woman who just called me?"

Nate nodded. "We dated my senior year of college and I guess since then she's changed her name." Which had Nate curious. Actually, he had more questions than answers when it came to her. Like how had she ended up in Cincinnati. After graduation, she'd planned to start law school. Why wasn't she practicing law somewhere?

Still a beautiful woman, her exotic eyes that used to be his weakness held a hint of sadness he wasn't used to seeing on her.

Nate sighed, feeling like scum for kicking her out. He acted like a punk kid instead of the chief financial officer of a multi-million dollar organization.

"Ahh, so that's it. She booted your ass to the curb and your feelings are still hurt," Nick taunted and sat in one of the chairs in front of the desk. "You do realize that was like a hundred years ago, right?"

"Man, whatever."

Nick burst out laughing, gone was the scowl he'd been wearing when he charged into the office. "Your ass got dumped," he said as if he couldn't believe it.

Nate wasn't ever going to live this moment down. They both had it easy when it came to attracting the opposite sex. Getting dumped wasn't an everyday occurrence. For Nate, he prided himself on treating women special. So why had he let his wounded ego dictate his behavior earlier? He was better than that. No woman, no matter what she'd done, deserved to be talked to like he'd done.

"I can't believe it. My brother, the self-proclaimed God's gift to women, got his ass handed to him," Nick cracked, cutting into Nate's thoughts.

"Need I remind you of what happened with Sumeera?" Nate looked at his brother pointedly and Nick slowly sobered.

"That was different."

"Was it? I remember her kicking you to the curb because you couldn't commit and—"

"And I eventually closed the deal." He wiggled his ring finger at Nate, and the overhead light bounced off the inlay of diamonds in the platinum band. "Not only are we happily married, but I got a gorgeous daughter out of the deal. What about you? You've been on fifty million dates, but haven't settled down. Why is that, huh?"

Nate remained quiet. Considering the number of women who'd crossed his path, there had only been one who stirred something within him. One who he would've done anything for, and one who...

"Wait." Nick sat forward and leaned his tattooed forearms on the desk. "So this woman, this Kayla or Liberty person, was the one. Was she the reason you were so jacked up after graduation? I always wondered about the mystery woman. If she meant that much to you, how is it that we never met her?"

After graduating high school, Nick stuck around Cincinnati. He went through a sheet metal apprenticeship while attending college with every intention of running the family business one day. Nate took a different path, wanting to experience life outside of Ohio. Attending Northwestern gave him the taste of freedom he had craved.

"We didn't date long," he finally said.

Nick lifted a questioning brow. "Yet, you were together long enough to fall in love with her."

Nate ran his hand down his face and lunged out of his seat. He turned to the window behind his desk and stared out at the employee parking lot. Only one person really knew of Kayla then and that was his father, Lewis.

Nate remembered when he had called his father for advice. Things between him and Kayla were getting serious, and Nate wanted some direction regarding next steps with her. Lewis, always the voice of reason mainly listened, asked a few questions then told Nate to follow his heart. And when Kayla walked away, Nate hadn't planned to tell anyone, but Lewis felt something was wrong. He had taken Nate, Nick, and a few of their cousins to Vegas. When Nate and Lewis were alone, Nate had told him everything.

"Sometimes you just know. At the time, I thought she was the one," Nate said still staring outside looking at nothing in particular.

"What happened? Why'd you guys break up?" When Nate remained quiet, Nick continued. "Hey, if it's none of my business, just say so."

"It's none of your business."

"Well, as your brother, I'm making it my business. What happened between you two?"

Nate turned from the window, debating on how much to share as he leaned on the desk. Though the incident happened so many years ago, it felt like yesterday. Kayla had cornered him in the room where the graduates were gathered before the ceremony. Totally out of breath, she looked as if she'd just returned from running a marathon, claiming she needed to talk to him immediately. Fear that something was wrong with her, he had hustled her away from his classmates.

"She flew to Vegas and got married the day before graduation," Nate said with very little emotion. In mere minutes, she had shattered his heart and derailed his future plans that had included her.

Nick sat stunned. Eyes wide and mouth hanging open, seconds ticked by before he spoke. "Dayum! That's some jacked up shit! No wonder you're trippin'. But why didn't you tell me? You know I would've been there for you."

"Yeah, right after you laughed me out of town."

A smile wavered on Nick's lips, and Nate wished he hadn't told him anything. "What'd you do when she told you?"

Thinking about that day angered Nate all over again. "I told her to have a nice life…in so many words."

Nick grinned. "Yeah, I just bet you did. So—"

"The worst part was that she left me to marry a guy who verbally abused her. There was even once when I thought he was going to hit her. Isaac Culpepper," Nate said the man's name with disgust.

"Isaac Culpepper? Of *the* Culpeppers in Chicago?"

"That would be the one. He's a big-time lawyer, and if I'm not mistaken, oversees some of his family's businesses. They come from old money and have their hands in a little bit of everything." Which Nate presumed had something to do with Kayla hooking up with Culpepper despite how bad the bastard had treated her.

Nate recalled an encounter he'd had with Isaac after spotting the two arguing across the lawn near Kayla's dorm. It was when Isaac grabbed her by the front of the shirt that Nate saw red. He took off in a sprint, not stopping until his fist made contact with the man's jaw. They fought, rolling around on the ground until campus police yanked them apart. That day Nate didn't know if he'd get kicked out of school or end up in jail for assault. Neither happened, but before being taken away, Isaac had warned that payback was coming.

Isaac definitely ended up having the last laugh.

Nate's intercom buzzed, shaking him out of his reverie. He pressed the intercom button on his desk phone. "Yes."

"Sorry to bother you, Nate, but is Nick with you?" the receptionist asked.

"Yeah, what's up, Tam?" Nick toyed with the golf ball paperweight their mother had given Nate after returning from Palm Springs.

"I've been calling you. Why aren't you answering your cell phone?" Tammy fussed.

"My battery died and I haven't had a chance to charge it. Why, what's going on?"

"Sumeera's been trying to reach you. She says it's not important, but she wants you to call her."

Nick stood. "Will do. Thanks."

"And Nate," the receptionist hurried to say.

"Yes?"

"Your nine o'clock appointment confirmed for tomorrow."

"All right. Thanks, Tammy."

Nate's cell phone vibrated on the desk and he glanced at the screen. Groaning he pushed decline. A second later, it rang again and he wasn't surprised to see the same person calling.

"Who are you avoiding?" Nick asked.

"Angel."

Nick folded his arms across his chest. "I thought you told her you weren't interested."

"I did, but she's not getting the message." Nate rubbed the side of his forehead. Angel Harris might be drop dead gorgeous with a good job as a sales executive for a beverage company, but this angel was turning into a devil. "We went out a few times, which was my first mistake. I knew she wasn't wrapped too tight after the second date, but I thought I was being too critical."

"You probably were. No one ever seems to be good enough."

"Anyway, after the third or fourth date, when she started talking about *our* wedding, as if we were engaged or something, I knew I had to move on."

"See this is what I've warned you about. All women can't handle the Jenkins charm," he said seriously and Nate laughed.

"Man, shut up. She'll get tired of calling eventually."

"You think ignoring her is a good idea? If something is mentally wrong with her, she might do something crazy."

"I'm not sure if she really has problems or was just messing with me regarding the whole wedding nonsense. I'm not too worried. Angel's job has her traveling a lot and she's out of town more than she's in town. I doubt if she's a nutcase."

Nick shrugged. "All right, well if you turn up missing we'll start with her."

Nate chuckled. "Yeah you do that. Now, I need to get back to work." Nate pulled the documents he'd been reading earlier closer.

"Okay. I want to hear more about your girl, but—"

"She's not my girl." She's a beautiful woman, he wanted to add but didn't bother.

"Well, Kayla…or Liberty, or whatever name she goes by. Nate, seriously though, we can't pass up this opportunity with LCA. You need to figure out a way to work with her."

Nate shook his head. "I'm not working with her. I also think it's not a good idea to go with LCA if they have her heading up this project. I don't trust her."

"You're punkin' out because of a girl?"

"She's not a girl!"

"Well, woman. You're not only screwing up this opportunity, but you're running from a woman." Nick stared at him, as if that would get Nate to change his mind. "Now I've heard everything. Poker night can't get here soon enough. The guys are going to eat this shit up."

Once a month they got together with a few of their cousins to play cards. The last thing Nate needed was to become the butt of their ribbing. They lived for crap like this, and it would be a first for him to be on the receiving end of their jokes.

"Fine. I'll call her and let her know that going forward, I'll be the contact person," Nick said. "We're not letting your personal issues get in the way of millions."

"Wait," Nate said just as Nick grabbed the doorknob. He had never let his personal business get in the way of work and he wasn't going to start now. "I'll talk to her."

A slow smile lifted the corner of Nick's mouth. "What changed your mind?"

"You. No way I'm letting you near our books. I also can't let you hold this project over my head for the rest of my life."

Besides, Nate was curious about the new Kayla…no, Liberty. Hell, he didn't know if he'd ever be able to see her as anyone other than Kayla, the girl he had fallen in love with in college. And if the sadness in her eyes was any indication, that fairytale life she thought she'd have thirteen years ago didn't end with a happily ever after.

Nate tapped his fingers against the desk. Maybe working with her wouldn't be all bad. If nothing else, he'd get to show her what she missed out on.

Chapter Four

Liberty stood in front of the full-length mirror second-guessing her outfit. She kept telling herself that she wasn't trying to impress Nate, but if she was honest, that's exactly what she was trying to do. After three changes, she'd finally settled on a flowy white blouse with bell sleeves, skinny black pants, and three-inch heels. Professional, yet stylish. Still, facing Nate again and not knowing what to expect had her on the verge of freaking out.

"Just relax and keep it professional," she told herself and blew out an anxious breath, willing the tightness in her chest to subside. Seeing Nate again had rocked her. All the old feelings came rushing back and Liberty's heart broke all over again. Leaving him had been the hardest thing she'd ever done in her life and if given the opportunity to do it over again, she would definitely make different choices. But there was nothing she could do about that now. That was in the past and she vowed to leave it all there.

She headed to the dining area of her tiny apartment for her laptop bag, and tried not to think about how different her life had turned out. Living in a penthouse with unobstructed 360-degree views of Chicago was a far cry from the one-bedroom apartment she lived in now. Gazing out the window at a brick building with an alley between them was a reminder of the changes in her life.

Stuffing the company's laptop and a notepad into the bag, she glanced around at the tiny, but tidy space. Her apartment was so small the kitchen, dining area, and living room were two steps from each other. This was all she could afford on her tight budget, but it sure beat the homeless shelter she'd been forced to live in only months earlier.

It's home.

The baby blue and brown color scheme was warm and inviting despite the sparse décor in the furnished apartment. She had moved in three weeks ago, and had finally unpacked the last box. It wasn't like she had a lot of belongings. Her ex-husband made sure she only left with what she'd come into the marriage with, and she was fine with that. All she wanted was out of that love-less, dysfunctional relationship.

"Don't start thinking about that asshole," she said into the quietness of the space. It had been over a year since they had separated and six months since their divorce had been finalized. The past year of searching for work, living on one meal a day, and barely keeping a roof over her head would go down as one of the worst years of her life. Some days she still couldn't believe that the man who she once thought of as a friend, the one who had vowed to take care of her until death, had turned out to be a monster.

"An arrogant, misogynistic monster is a more accurate description," she mumbled.

Her cell phone rang before she could add to the list of deplorable adjectives that described Isaac Culpepper. When her phone rang again, she hurried to the bedroom and grabbed it from the bedside table. A smile tugged at her lips seeing her sister's photo on the screen.

"Demi, you're turning into a mother hen. You don't have to check on me every day."

"Yeah, whatever. Are you ready to face that Nubian god again?"

Liberty chuckled. "I have to stop telling you everything."

"Don't you dare. You went years keeping me in the dark with all that you were going through. Now we have a deal. We talk about everything. That means *everything*. Got it?"

"Yeah, yeah, yeah. I've got it."

After Liberty had finally left her husband, she held off telling Demi the news. Her sister knew a little about what she'd gone through, but not everything. The last thing Liberty wanted was to hear the *I-told-you-so* or be questioned about why she'd stayed so long. Nor did she want her sister's pity. Ostracized in Chicago's business world by her ex-husband, Liberty not only struggled to find work, but her self-esteem had taken a significant hit. Yet, she had suffered in silence for months, barely able to keep a roof over her head and food on the table.

The day she had finally broken down and called her sister, her life started turning around. Demi and her fiancé, Alan, flew to Chicago and helped relocate her to Cincinnati. Despite all she'd been through in Chicago, it had been hard to leave the city she loved. But the move probably saved her life.

"And how are you…feeling?" her sister asked carefully.

The hesitation in the question let Liberty know that Demi wasn't referring to the job. Her sister feared she suffered from some type of depression. Liberty's life had never been perfect, but normally she could pick herself up and dust herself off. It hadn't been as easy this time. However, after some serious self-talk over the last couple of days, she was encouraged that this second chance at the life she desired was on track.

"I'm fine, Demi. You have enough on your plate. Don't worry about me. Besides, you should be getting ready for your trip to Philadelphia." She and Alan were heading out of town to visit his family for a few days.

"But I'm never too busy for you."

"I know, and I feel the same about you." Liberty glanced at the clock on the nightstand. "Okay, I don't want to be late. So I need to get going."

"Alright, but if Nate acts like a jerk again, put him in his place. You don't have to take crap from him."

Liberty laughed. "Listen to you trying to sound all tough. I think Nate and I will be fine, at least professionally." Personally, Liberty didn't think he would ever forgive her for what she'd done, and that was something she would have to live with. However, maybe he would eventually come around and give her a chance to explain herself. Maybe.

*

By the time Liberty arrived at Jenkins & Sons Construction, her nerves were all over the place. Early in her career, when she did project management at a law firm she once worked at, she had all the confidence in the world when meeting with clients. Now, not so much. Yet, she was determined to prove to herself that she was still the beautiful, intelligent, independent woman she'd been then.

"Hi, may I help you?" the receptionist from the other day with short dreadlocks, friendly eyes, and a bright smile, greeted when Liberty walked into the building.

"Hi, I'm Liberty Stewart. I'm here to see Nathaniel Moore...uh, I mean Jenkins."

"Okay, I'll let him know you're here."

Liberty strolled to the end of the receptionist's counter, her attention on the wall of photographs that she had missed the other day. She had just acquired the assignment the week before, but what she'd learned of the company impressed her. Family owned and operated, they were one of the largest construction companies in the city, fourth to LCA. She took in the architectural photographs, impressed by some of the work they'd done in the state. According to her supervisor, LCA didn't often partner with other construction companies, but due to stipulations in the State's request for proposals, they were making an exception. The State wanted the project to be as inclusive as possible, insisting any company that submitted bids have a certain number of minorities.

"Ms. Stewart."

Liberty whirled around, rocking unsteadily on her heels at hearing the sound of Nate's voice.

Good, Lord. Give me strength. This man…

He'd been a sight the other day, but today he looked like a sexy, powerful executive ready to close on a deal. Gone were the casual polo shirt and dress pants. Today he sported a dark-blue suit with faint pinstripes, a gray dress shirt, and a tie that pulled the whole ensemble together. If dressing to kill wasn't enough torture, his heady scent of soap with a hint of sandalwood floated the short distance between them and was sure to do her in.

How the heck was she going to focus on work when he looked and smelled so good?

"Tammy, is anyone using conference room D?" Nate asked the receptionist.

"Not at the moment, but Liam has it reserved for 11 o'clock."

Nate glanced at his watch. "That only gives us a half an hour." He turned to Liberty. "Let's start in there."

Snapping out of her trance-like state, Liberty realized what he'd said. If he thought thirty-minutes would be enough time to go over all that they needed to cover, he was sadly mistaken. Not wanting to voice the thought in front of the other woman, Liberty followed him. With a confident swagger she didn't remember him having in college, Nate moved down the hall like a man in charge.

"In here," he said extending his hand in the direction of the open door to a small conference room. Liberty entered before him.

"Nate, we're going to need more than thirty minutes." She set her laptop bag on the floor next to the closest chair.

"You might be right, but for what I want to discuss right now, it won't take that long. Have a seat." He pulled out the chair for her, and then he unbuttoned his suit jacket before joining her at the small table. "I owe you an apology."

Stunned, Liberty sat up straighter. Though she felt he owed her one, she'd never expected him to apologize. All her years of marriage to Isaac, enduring his evilness and not once did he say *I'm sorry*. He made it seem as if every negative situation they experienced together was prompted by her. This was another reminder of how he and Nate were two very different men.

"About the other day," he started, but paused.

Nate ran his hand over his mouth and down his goatee. Liberty wasn't sure what the hesitation was about. Maybe he was trying to find the right words. His steady gaze held hers for the longest time until he continued.

"In representing this company, I have carried myself in a professional manner at all times. The other day my behavior and attitude toward you were deplorable, and for that I apologize. Though my personal feelings toward you remain the same. I don't trust you. But since J & S has decided to work with LCA, I will do my best to keep our interactions strictly professional."

Well, damn. He's not going to make this easy.

That wall he'd built to protect himself from her was strong and unyielding. And the coldness in his tone had her rethinking her decision to return. In hindsight, maybe she should have talked with her boss about reassigning the project.

No. I need this opportunity to show LCA what I can accomplish.

She also needed to prove to herself that she wasn't a failure, and that she still had what it took to be a success in anything she set out to do.

Liberty stared down at her hands as she gathered her thoughts. A bit torn by his reception, she wasn't quite sure how to respond. She was there to do a job. Yet, a part of her had hoped they could make peace and then create the best proposal the State ever reviewed.

One out of two wasn't bad.

Returning her attention to Nate, she straightened her shoulders and said, "Thanks for that half-ass apology. Let's get started."

Chapter Five

Nate almost smiled at her fake bravado. She wasn't fooling anyone. His words hit the mark. He wasn't trying to make her uncomfortable but... Okay, maybe he was trying to get under her skin. He wanted her to experience a little of the hurt he still felt from the way she'd ended things between them. If that made him a jerk, oh well. Yes, he was sorry for the way he'd treated her the other day, but he meant what he said. He didn't trust her.

"We can discuss next steps in my office," Nate said.

They walked up the stairs in silence, but Nate was very much aware of Liberty's long, sexy strides and the hypnotic sway of her hips. He wanted to maintain some emotional and physical distance from her, but she wasn't making it easy. How the hell was he supposed to ignore the way the low-cut blouse revealed just enough cleavage to capture his attention. And those damn pants. She had the perfect, curvaceous body for snug fitting pants and these highlighted her firm thighs and round ass. But it was the arousing scent of lavender radiating off her that had him tempted to do something stupid. Like press his nose against her long, graceful neck to get a better whiff.

Dammit. Why'd he have to still be attracted to her? Why couldn't everything about her disgust him?

Temperature rising along with his frustration, he pushed open his office door, ready to hurry this along. "We can work at the table in the corner."

Nate growled internally as she strolled across his office, adding more hip action to her walk. Suggesting they work in his personal space was turning into a bad idea, but it was more convenient. He wasn't totally sure what information he'd need access to, but anything they could possibly need was in reach.

After closing the door, Nate took a seat at the table and studied her while she organized the paperwork. The shadows under her eyes were more pronounced than they were during her last visit. Had she lost sleep the last couple of days the way he had?

"So tell me," he started, "why the name change? I didn't really know Isaac Culpepper, but I would assume someone like him would want you to carry his name."

Lips thinned in annoyance, she met his gaze. "Nate, I think it best we stay away from personal questions and focus on the job at hand. My name has no bearing on us getting this project done."

"Why so secretive about the name?" Seeing her the other day had totally caught him off guard, but it was the new identity that had him puzzled. Not knowing why she didn't go by Kayla Jackson any longer was driving him crazy.

"Why do you want to know? You've made it clear that this is a working relationship. Nothing else." She went back to paper shuffling.

"I don't know if I can stop calling you Kayla," he admitted.

"That's too bad because I'll only be answering to Liberty."

This time Nate did smile, not that she would've notice since the paperwork had her full attention. In college, she'd been one of the sweetest people he'd ever met, and she had a dry sense of humor that peeked out occasionally. One of many things he once loved about her. Shortly after they had parted ways, there were times when he could still hear her laugh, or recall one of her sassy retorts. It was those small things that had made him miss her all the more.

She turned the top page of the stack of papers around and pointed. "I'm thinking with the overview section we'll each come up with a description for our companies. Then I'll combine the two to make them complement each other."

"So how is married life?"

"Tell me about Jenkins & Sons," she said without missing a beat.

"That good, huh?" Nate didn't miss the way she balled the fingers of her left hand into a fist. "You should be able to find information about the company on our website."

He picked up the thick proposal packet wondering how many hours and days of torture he'd have to endure working with her.

"But I'm asking you. Tell me something that I wouldn't find on the site."

Nate flipped the page over to peruse the other side and didn't have to look at Kayla to feel the intense heat of her stare.

"How long have you and your husband been in Cincinnati? And how did you get Mr. Deep Pockets to leave Chicago?"

"Nate."

"Kayla."

She huffed and typed something into her laptop. For a moment, he thought she would ignore him for the rest of their time together.

But then she asked, "Besides you, will anyone else be overseeing the project at Jenkins & Sons?"

"Probably," Nate said simply, folding his arms across his chest.

"Who else should I list?"

Nate shrugged. "I don't know who'll want to be listed. Just put me down."

"What about Nick? He's excited about the venture. Actually, maybe I should be working with him. At least then we could be making some progress, and I wouldn't have to deal with your negative attitude."

Nate fumed, but kept his mouth shut, not wanting to say anything that would have him apologizing again.

For the next hour, they worked through the first few sections of the document and Nate could feel the tension bouncing off of the new Kayla. His half-ass answers were getting to her, but he couldn't help himself. At first, he found perverse pleasure in challenging her at every turn, but the more time he spent with her, the more irritated he became. There was no way he'd be able to work with this woman without them addressing their issues. Now that she was back in his life, he needed an explanation of why she had walked away from him.

While she typed information into her laptop, Nate stood and moved to the front of his desk. He leaned against it and folded his arms across his chest.

"I have a question for you. Instead of LCA partnering with a minority company, why don't they just start hiring more minorities?"

"Unfortunately, I haven't been with the company long. I don't know their hiring practices yet. I think that's a good question th—"

"What *do* you know, Kayla? Every other question I have asked you, you say *good question* or *I'll find out*. Why are you even on this project?"

"Don't call me Kayla." She pursed her lips and gripped her pen tighter. Instead of answering his question, she jotted down something on the notepad next to her laptop. "I think we've done enough today. We should coordinate a few more meetings over the next two weeks. What's your schedule look like?"

Nate released a long drawn out sigh. "Why don't I just call you when I'm avail—"

"Dammit, Nate!" She threw her pen across the room and lunged out of the chair. "Quit acting like an ass. I'm sick of it! Are you going to be a jerk every time we meet?"

Anger crept through Nate's body. "Excuse me?"

"You heard me! First you give me that lame-ass apology, and for the past hour, you've been acting like a two-year-old. If your organization doesn't want to partner with LCA, just say so. Don't keep wasting my damn time!"

"Hold up." He pushed away from the desk. "My apology was sincere, but you're right. I don't want to be here with you. Just because we have agreed to work on the Unity Tower project doesn't mean that I have to enjoy our time together."

"What do you want from me?" she pleaded, some of the fight leaving her.

"All I want is for us to finish this proposal as soon as possible so that I don't have to be in your presence."

She shook her head and started shoving items into her bag. "I can't do this. I'll let LCA know that you guys aren't interested in working with us."

"Now you wait a minute. You're the one who's getting all sensitive about everything I say. Why is that? Is your conscience bothering you? Are you feeling guilty about being a lying bitch?"

She spun on her heels and her hand ripped across his face, the sound echoing throughout the room.

Fury roared through Nate. "Don't you *ever* put your hands on me again!"

"And don't you *ever* call me a bitch," she rasped, emotion clogging her words as her chest heaved up and down. "This project might not mean anything to you, but it means everything to me. I would rather us finish it successfully, but since that doesn't seem possible, let's just end this now. I've been fighting for most of my life and I don't have the energy to fight you too. More importantly, I will not stand here and let you call me out of my name.

Some of Nate's anger subsided as he thought about what he'd said to her and took in her reaction. A shimmer of tears shone in her eyes, but she hurried and looked away.

Shit. I'm an idiot.

He had definitely crossed the line, but the asshole inside of him wouldn't apologize. And what did she mean about fighting for most of her life?

Without looking at him she said, "You're rehashing something that happened over a decade ago. You need to let it go and move on."

"I have moved on," he lied, "but trusting you is something I'll never be able to do."

Liberty brought her hands to her face and growled into her palms. "Why can't you just let it go?"

"Because…" He rubbed his forehead in frustration. "*I— I can't.*"

∗

Liberty's heart squeezed in anguish as she realized she had hurt him more than she originally thought. Unfortunately, nothing she could do or say would be enough to express how sorry she was for walking away from what they once had.

Pushing down the emotion threatening to explode within her, she hurried to pack her belongings.

"Nate, we both have a job to do," she finally said but kept her head down hoping her voice sounded stronger than she felt. "What's it going to take for you to put the past behind us and focus on the here and now?"

"I need answers," he responded quietly.

Liberty raised her gaze to his. The hurt in his eyes sliced open an old wound and shattered the last shred of her control. The anger and fight in him had dissipated.

"What do you want me to say?" she asked, unable to catch the slight whimper that slipped through. "Do you want me to admit that walking away from you was the biggest mistake I've ever made? Do you want me to tell you that my life has been one huge failure after another? Do you want me to say that my world has been *hell* without you in it?" Her breaths came hard and ragged as her chest tightened. She didn't want to break down in front of him, but revisiting that painful time in her life was never easy.

Nate opened his mouth to speak, but nothing came out. Stuffing one hand into his pants pocket, he used the other to rub the back of his neck.

"You want to know why I walked away?" She searched for the right words to give him some idea of her frame of mind when they went their separate ways. "Marrying Isaac was the only way to save my family. It was the only way to keep a roof over their head and food on the table," she choked out. Her heart ached as she remembered her parents' struggles. "While I was growing up, I can't tell you how many cans of Pork & Beans I was forced to eat. Or dry tuna sandwiches that I had to choke down if I didn't want to go hungry. Or maybe you want to hear about the evictions or how many days we sat in the dark. I had to do my homework by candlelight because my parents couldn't afford to keep the lights on."

"Kay—Liberty." Nate moved closer and she took a step back, tears blurring her vision. If he touched her, there was no way she'd be able to say what she needed him to know.

"Do you honestly think I wanted to leave you? Walk away from what we had? Leave the only man I've ever loved?" Liberty covered her mouth, trying not to yield to the sobs clawing their way up her throat. She swallowed hard, fighting to pull herself together. "No one, Nate, and I mean *no one* has ever made me feel as loved and cherished as you did. There hasn't been a day that has gone by that I haven't regretted my decision to leave you. Is…is that what you want to hear?"

Her heart raced and ached at the same time. And to her horror, tears rolled down her cheeks faster than she could swipe them away. God, the last thing she wanted to do was cry, but the ache in her chest was overwhelming. She had so many regrets and it was as if all of them were coming to the forefront and strangling what little peace she had.

"Stop…baby, just…don't cry." Nate reached for her and Liberty held her hands out in front of herself to halt him. That same compassion she used to feel from him, and see in his eyes during their tender moments, radiated off of him. But she needed to keep some distance between them in order to finish before the memories suffocated her.

"Was it bad that I believed Isaac when he told me that if I was his wife, my mother's enormous hospital bills would be paid in full? He promised me that my family would never have to worry about being evicted again. If that weren't enough, he told me that I'd never want for anything ever again. It might sound shallow, but was I wrong to go after the *one* chance I had to help me and my family dig out of poverty?"

Liberty blindly grasped the top of the chair and used her free hand to wipe her eyes and face. She hadn't broken down like this in a long time. Finding it hard to catch her breath, her hand went to her chest as if that would help get air into her lungs. The harder she tried to calm down, the tougher it was to breathe.

"Come here." Nate eased her into his arms, unwilling to let her pull away this time. He was at a loss. Caught off guard by Liberty's admission, he didn't know what to say. He just held on as her body trembled against him. Unable to help himself, he placed a kiss on her temple, hoping he was offering some comfort. Her lavender scent was even more potent than when she arrived.

To Nate's surprise, Liberty buried her face in the crook of his neck and wrapped her arms around his waist, gripping the back of his shirt as if it were a lifeline. She felt so perfect in his arms. How many times had he dreamed of holding her again, talking late into the night about their future, or just being in her presence? But not like this. Not with her crying and sharing some disturbing revelations.

41

Liberty sagged against his chest, and her sobs quieted. "I can't believe I let you make me cry." She tried to laugh, but it came out more like a whimper.

"I'm sorry," Nate murmured close to her ear. "You're right. I've been a total ass and—"

"Nate, will you tell this bonehead th…" Martina slid to a stop just inside the office with their cousin, Liam, hot on her heels.

Liberty stiffened in Nate's arm and then tried pulling away, but he didn't let go. Martina had the worst timing ever. A carpenter by trade, she worked closely with his brother in overseeing many of the company's jobs. Liam was the architect in the family. He mostly worked from home, but came into the office once or twice a week.

"Well, what do we have here?" Martina smirked. Nate glared at her. She was a pain in the ass on most days, and he had often threatened to kill her. Right now he was more tempted than ever.

"MJ, what did I tell you about barging into my office? Whatever you guys want, it can wait. Close my door back on your way out."

"Actually, I'd rather stick around and find out why you're hugged up with—"

"We're outta here." Liam grabbed Martina's arm and pulled her out of the room, closing the door behind them. Nate could still hear them arguing in the hallway, which wasn't unusual with Martina around.

"I apologize," Nate said to Liberty, releasing her when she pushed against his chest. "Apparently I need to start locking my door."

Barely able to look at him, Liberty flashed a wobbly smile and went to her bag. "I should go. I wish I could say that I've never been so embarrassed in all of my life," she mumbled on a shaky exhale. "Unfortunately, this is the story of my life."

"What do you mean?" Nate still had so many questions.

She shook her head and waved him off. "Never mind. I'm sorry about…everything. I didn't want to hurt you, Nate. Please know that nothing happened between Isaac and me while you and I were together. I wasn't…I didn't…I wasn't *with* him while I was with you."

Knowing she hadn't cheated on him with Isaac should have made Nate feel better. All it did was create more questions. Questions he couldn't ask her while she was in this condition.

"I won't pretend I understand exactly why you walked away, or what you've been through, but I'm sorry…again. I've been a complete jerk."

"I'm sorry too for blowing up and…and I shouldn't have slapped you. I have never done anything like that before." Her hand flew to her mouth to hold back a sob and more tears pooled in her eyes. He felt bad that he had provoked her, especially since she was so upset about hitting him. "I'm not sure what came over me."

"I deserved the slap. I shouldn't have said those things to you. As for all that you've told me, seemed you needed to get a few things off your chest."

"Maybe, but I shouldn't have…not like this. Not here."

True. It was never a good idea to bring personal issues to the work place, and he hated the way he'd acted. There had definitely been a better way to handle the situation. Had he not been acting like a damn fool, he would have suggested they meet for lunch or go somewhere to talk. They had never fought before, always able to talk through their disagreements. The only good thing that had come from her break down was that he had needed to hear everything she'd said. Now what to do with the information was another story.

"I know right now my word means nothing to you, but I promise going forward I'll be totally professional," he said.

"Thanks. I'll call you in a couple of days to set something up."

He was almost afraid to let her leave, fearing that she'd disappear again. "If I don't hear from you soon, Liberty, I'll contact you."

She hesitated for a moment and then nodded. When she rubbed her head, and glanced around as if not knowing what to do or say next, Nate asked, "Are you sure you're okay to drive?"

"I'll be fine, thank you." She started for the door, but stopped and pulled an envelope from the side of her bag. "Oh and um…happy birthday."

Chapter Six

"Ca—can I get another one?" Liberty asked, holding up her empty glass. She set it down when the bartender acknowledged her from the end of the bar with a nod.

A co-worker had told her about Teddy's Bar & Grill, saying it was a good place to drink and think. After the day she'd had, Liberty had no intention of thinking, only drinking which was a new experience. On occasion, she had a glass of wine, but hadn't had any hard liquor since a frat party she attended in college. After one drink and watching her roommates party to the point of throwing up, Liberty had vowed then never to get drunk.

Yet, here she was, at the point of having one too many, but not caring. She wasn't driving, and she still had her faculties. One more drink wouldn't hurt. Besides, it beat going home and staring at the TV. All that would lead to was her thinking about a certain tall, dark, and handsome man who she made a fool of herself in front of earlier. Nate probably thought she was a total loser. Only a loser would marry one man when she loved another, right?

Liberty shook her head. "Too little, too late."

Maybe a few more drinks could dull all of her senses. Heck, if there was a way to wipe her memory, she would go for it.

"Bartender!" she called out again, glad to see him making his way back to her.

"Don't you think you've had enough?" he asked. He looked like a badass rocker, with a little scruff on his face and long, dark blond hair pulled into a ponytail at his nape. He had the prettiest hazel eyes Liberty had ever seen on a man. "How about some coffee instead?"

"I haven't even got a buzz yet. I think I can handle a couple of more. Just keep them coming."

"I don't know, sweetheart. You might not be falling-off-the-barstool drunk, but you're slurring some of your—"

"Go ahead, Jaz. Give the lady another one on me. I'll make sure she doesn't drive home," a man said. He was casually dressed with fair skin, freckles around his nose, and a crooked grin. Sitting on the barstool next to her, his smile widened.

"Yeah, Jaz. Give me ano—another one. I wo—won't drive," Liberty slurred. "I can't. My car di—died." Yet another reason to drown her sorrows with alcohol. If she didn't have bad luck, she wouldn't have any luck at all. Lately whenever she took two steps forward, she got knocked back four. She wasn't sure what she'd do about her car situation now. Only paying nine hundred dollars for the vehicle, more items didn't work than did, including the radio that only turned on when she hit a bump. At least the vehicle had gotten her around for a while.

"All right, one more, but I'm keeping an eye on you." Seconds later Jaz set a whiskey neat in front of her.

"Thanks," she said and then turned to her new friend and lifted the glass. "Thank you."

"You're welcome. I'm Bruce, by the way, and you are?"

"Just a per—person tryin' to forget her tro—troubles." Liberty sipped her drink, uninterested in conversation.

Bruce didn't take the hint. For the next twenty minutes, she heard stories about his multiple printing stores, the house he was having built, and the new car he had outside. If he thought those things would impress her, he was mistaken.

She was so over *stuff*. If she ever opened her heart to a man again, it would be for love. Not money or material things.

"We're practically best friends considering the amount of time we've spent together. Are you ever going to tell me your name?"

Liberty shook her head. She was done with men. Staring into the amber liquid she recalled some of the mean things her ex-husband had done to her over the years. And then there were the lies. The awful lies he often spewed about her being an addict. She had never touched drugs in her life. Even when times were unbearable, indulging in narcotics was never a consideration. Neither was alcohol.

But tonight, Liberty just didn't care. She wanted to wash all the bad memories away.

She slammed back the rest of the whiskey then closed her eyes, wincing at the burn in the back of her throat.

Dang that's strong.

She pushed the drink away and rested her head on her forearms on top of the bar.

"Are you okay?" Bruce asked.

No, she wasn't okay. Had she stopped at the strawberry mojito before switching to whiskey, maybe her head wouldn't be swimming, but no. She just had to take the edge off of her lousy day.

Instead of admitting to Bruce that she probably wasn't okay, she said, "I'm fine."

"Want another one?" he asked.

Liberty opened her eyes, but closed them again when the room started spinning. Okay, maybe tossing back the rest of the drink had been a bad idea.

*

"Here's to another year of life, bro," Nick said tapping his beer bottle to Nate's glass of scotch. Cheers went around the table as the other men followed suit. Despite not being in the mood for partying, Nate was trying not to ruin the evening for his brother. He and Nick were celebrating their thirty-sixth birthday with a few guys, mostly their cousins.

Normally they'd be sitting around a poker table talking trash on a Friday night. Instead, they stopped off for a drink after dinner to wrap up their celebration.

After work, some of his family had met at his parents' house. For as long as Nate could remember, his mother had insisted on cooking him and Nick a celebratory dinner on their birthday. Even at their age, they looked forward to their mother spoiling them with their favorite dishes and catering to them on their special day. Once dinner was over, the guys had suggested they stop by Teddy's Bar & Grill for a couple of drinks.

Unfortunately, Nate couldn't focus on the lively bunch. Ever since Liberty strolled in and settled at the bar, his attention had been on her. From the moment she walked out of his office hours ago, he'd been worried. Mentally kicking himself for letting her leave when she was still upset. He had called her twice, each time getting her voicemail. Now, there she was sitting across the room drinking more than she probably should.

What he really wanted was to talk to her, question her more about some of the things she'd mentioned in his office.

"Do you honestly think I wanted to leave you? Walk away from what we had? Leave the only man I've ever loved?"

Her words rattled him. Did that mean that she had never loved her ex-husband? The snippets she'd given him of the last thirteen years of her life weren't enough. Even more questions about her plagued him. Nate didn't know how or when, but he planned to get answers.

"I thought you two had kissed and made up. How long are you going to sit here staring at her?" Nick asked, talking loud enough to be heard over the latest Nicki Minaj song thumping through the speaker not too far from their table.

Nate didn't have to ask who Nick had been talking to. Not only was Martina a pain in the ass on most days, but she was also the busy-body, know-it-all in the family who inserted herself into everyone's business.

"Yeah, Mr. Lady's Man. Put us all out of the misery of your funky attitude and go to the woman. You know you want to," Jerry taunted. "Hell, I still can't believe there was a woman out in the world who managed to get our boy to let down that guard around his heart. I know many a woman who has tried."

His cousins and brother continued talking about him and his serial dating behavior as if he wasn't sitting there. Nate didn't care. He could admit that he had only ever loved one woman. It wasn't until the past year or so that he noticed his dating habits. After a few outings with a woman, he soon tired of them and moved on to the next. Even though he desired marriage and a family, he was careful never to lead any of them on if he didn't feel a connection soon after they started dating. Now he wondered if he would ever love another woman the way he once loved the one sitting on the other side of the room.

Without taking his gaze from Liberty, Nate brought his scotch to his lips. The slight burn of it going down his throat did nothing to squelch the desire to go to her. After her break down in his office, he was pretty sure she'd had enough of him for one day. But like back in college, whenever she was near, his senses went on high alert. Like a homing device, his gaze had always zeroed in on her. Tonight was no different.

"Okay, birthday boys, what else can I get you guys?" Frenchy, the server asked.

Many of the Jenkins family were regulars and like the staff knew most of them, the family knew the staff. Usually whenever Nate stopped by Teddy's, Francesca, who preferred to be called Frenchy, was there. She was an accountant by day and a barmaid at night.

"Rumor has it Jerry's buying this round." She winked at Jerry, knowing she would get a rise out of him.

"Come here, girl," Jerry said, pulling her to his side, his long arm going easily around her thick waist. "Who told you I was buying the next round?"

"I just figured it was your turn." The server whispered something in his ear, and with the wicked grin on Jerry's face, Nate could almost imagine what she was promising his cousin. Frenchy, a plus size woman who always looked pulled together, knew she was Jerry's type physically. He only dated thick and curvy women. Yet, no matter how much she flirted, Jerry never asked her out, which baffled Nate. Jerry was a player and proud of it, chasing anything in a skirt, especially if she sported wide hips and big legs. Frenchy fit the bill.

"Frenchy, when you're done talking dirty to my cousin, I need a favor," Nate said, his attention back on Liberty and the man sitting next to her.

"Anything you want, honey. Since your cousin ain't giving me no play, I'm all yours." She moved away from Jerry and batted her long, false eyelashes at Nate. He couldn't help but chuckle. She didn't quit. She was determined to snag her a Jenkins man. Her words not his.

Nate stood slightly. He lowered his voice and moved close to her ear. "Tell Jaz to cut off the woman over there," he nodded toward Liberty, "the one with the white blouse talking to the bald guy. I'll cover her tab."

Franky shook her head. "Always the boy scout, huh, Nate? Looking out for another damsel in distress."

Nate didn't take offense to the boy scout comment. He never liked to see a woman taken advantage of and considering the number of drinks Liberty had consumed, that's exactly what could happen if she wasn't careful.

"All right, I'll tell him."

After taking his cousins' orders, Frenchy sauntered to the bar. Jaz, the bartender, glanced at him while she whispered in his ear and gave a slight nod in Nate's direction.

Liberty had been at the bar for the last forty minutes and was on her fourth drink. Yes, he had counted. She might have changed over the years, but Nate had a feeling she wasn't a drinker. At least she wasn't one when they attended college. Then again, there was so much he didn't know about her. But considering she was struggling to keep her head up, no doubt she had reached her limit.

"You, my brother, are a bleeding heart," Nick said, nudging Nate with his arm. "If you're so worried about the woman, go over there and take care of her."

"Maybe I wi…"

Nate's cell phone vibrated in his pants pocket. Pulling the device out he glanced at the screen and groaned.

Angel.

"I'll be back," he said to Nick who waved him off.

Angel had been blowing up his phone for the last couple of days and he had finally answered one of her calls last night. He thought he had made it clear, again, that he wasn't looking for anything serious with her.

"Hello," Nate answered against his better judgment and slid past a few people to get somewhere quieter. He stopped near a back booth where no one was sitting.

"Nate? Can you hear me?"

"Yeah, I can hear you. What's up?"

"Where are you?"

"Out. What do you want, Angel?"

"What do I want?" She chuckled, the low cackle grating on his nerves. "I want *you*. Why don't you stop by tonight?"

Nate shook his head. "Angel, we talked about this. I won't be stopping by your place. You won't be stopping by mine. I think it's best we move on. Go our separate ways. Date other people."

She sighed dramatically. "Nate, we have a good time when we're together. Why can't we hang out and see how things go?"

Nate glanced across the room at Liberty, thinking about the connection they once had. "Angel, I'm looking for something serious and I don't think I can have that with you."

"I want a serious relationship, too. That's why I've—"

"Angel, I'm sorry, but I'm just not interested in you. I don't know how else to make you understand that."

"You haven't even…"

Nate stood straighter, tuning out anything else Angel said. Jaz had caught his attention. Waving from the bar area, he pointed to where Liberty had been sitting.

Unease crept through Nate's body when he didn't see her or the guy who had been hovering over her. Nate's gaze searched the small dance floor and he didn't see her, but movement to his right caught his attention.

Even after all of these years, seeing another man's hands on Liberty was like taking a punch to the gut. He had no claims on her, but at the moment he wanted to decrease the space between them and yank the bastard's arm out of his socket.

The guy had a hold on her elbow urging her toward the front exit. Nate had never seen Liberty look so out of it. She could barely put one foot in front of the other.

"Angel, I have to go. Take care."

Nate shoved his phone into his pocket, bumping into people as he shouldered his way through a crowd that had formed not too far from the entrance. Liberty didn't know this man. And Nate knew that because the guy had sidle up to her after watching her from the end of the bar for the first thirty minutes after her arrival.

There was no way in hell he was letting her leave with the guy.

"Where do you think you're going with her?" Nate asked, blocking their path.

"Who the hell are you?" The man pulled her roughly against his body and Liberty sagged against him, her head dropping to his shoulder.

"I'm a friend of hers, and I can't let you take her out of here. Liberty," Nate called her name. Her eyes were partially closed, but seeing him, she blinked several times as if trying to figure out if he was really standing in front of her.

He reached for her hand. "Liberty, can you hear me?" He moved closer.

"Na—Nate," she whispered, barely able to hold her head up.

The man turned her away as if protecting a toy from getting taken. "Dude, get the hell away from us, and mind your own damn business."

"She is my business. So you need to let her go." Liberty slurred something else that Nate couldn't understand. "Do you want to leave with him?" Nate asked her.

She started to shake her head but stopped and grabbed it. "No. I'm…I'm so tired."

That was all Nate needed to hear. "Let. Her. Go," he growled through gritted teeth, his voice carrying a lethal edge as he held onto the hand Liberty extended to him. He didn't want to make a scene, but he would if it meant keeping them from walking out. It had been a long time since Nate took a swing at anyone.

"Is there a problem over here?" Jerry stepped into view to the right of Nate.

The man's eyes grew large. Jerry could be intimidating standing well over six feet tall. His muscular frame was like that of a bodybuilder's.

Nick approached from the left, and Nate figured the others were pretty close by as well. Rarely did any of them get into jams, but family first had been drilled into them since birth. Nate found it comforting to know they always had his back.

The guy holding onto Liberty looked from one to the other before glaring at Nate. "Shit. She ain't worth all of this." He shoved her against Nate and stormed away.

Liberty gripped the front of Nate's shirt tightly, her head resting heavily against his chest. "I'm sorry."

"I've got you, baby." Nate scooped her limp body into his arms and headed for the door.

Now, what to do with her.

Chapter Seven

Nate held Liberty close to his body as he carried her up the stairs to his guest room, relishing in how good she felt in his arms. He almost chuckled thinking that he had only carried a woman to bed, literally, twice in his life. Each of those times happened to be the same woman—Liberty.

Stepping onto the second-floor landing and heading down the long hallway, Nate wondered if bringing her to his house was a good idea. But where else could he take her? She had fallen asleep in his car before they even left the bar's parking lot. He'd been such a jerk each time they were together, he knew nothing about her except what little she revealed during her break down earlier. Since her driver's license still had a Chicago address, he had no clue where she lived. Did she have any family in town? Did she know anyone besides him?

More damn questions.

The only thing he knew for sure was that he was glad he'd been at Teddy's tonight. Anything could have happened to her. When Jaz had caught his attention, and nodded toward Liberty leaving with that guy, every protective instinct within Nate kicked into gear. He had no right to be so possessive, but there was no way he could let her walk out of that building with a random stranger.

Nate entered the semi-dark guest room, lit only by the moonlight shining through the window and casting a soft glow over the room. He gently deposited Liberty onto the queen-sized bed. The moment her body touched the mattress, she turned onto her side.

A smile touched his lips. Seeing her curl into the ball reminded him of how she used to sleep in that position when they were together. Except then her ass had always been rubbed up against his crotch.

Nate shook the memory free. No sense in going down that road. It was a lifetime ago.

He turned her onto her back. Carefully, he lifted her upper body in order to remove the small, over the shoulder purse from around her and placed it on the nightstand next to the bed. Her shoes were next. After setting them on the floor, Nate covered her with a lightweight blanket and stared down at her sleeping form. She was still one of the most beautiful women he'd ever known. She looked so peaceful and...tiny in the large bed. He had a sudden urge to kiss her tempting lips, but instead he pushed some of the strands of her disheveled hair away from her face. Taking in the softness of her features a feeling he couldn't identify lodged in his chest.

God, he missed her. Even being angry that she had walked away, there were so many times that he thought about her, wondered what she was up to, and if she was happy.

He didn't know how long he stood watching her. Tempted to camp out in the chair that sat in the corner to make sure she was all right, he nixed the idea. The last thing he needed was to catch feelings for her. Instead he closed the curtains and turned on the light in the attached bathroom just in case she woke in the middle of the night.

He headed for the door but stopped and glanced over his shoulder at his guest. After graduation, Nate thought he would never see her again. Now fate had brought her back into his life and he wanted to know everything about her.

"No time like the present," he mumbled as he headed downstairs. He made a cup of coffee and carried it to his office. When he set it in the corner on the desk, his cell phone vibrated.

Nate dug the device from his pocket before dropping down in his desk chair. "Hello."

"So, did you get sleeping beauty settled into your bed okay?" Nate didn't miss the humor in his brother's voice.

He brought the coffee mug up to his lips and took a tentative sip before responding. "Not that it's any of your business, but Liberty is not in my bed. She's in the guest room."

"Are you sure it was a good idea to take her to your house?"

"Nick, what else was I supposed to do? What would you have done?"

After a long hesitation, he said, "Probably the same thing. If she's new to town, I'm a little surprised she would go to a bar alone and then get drunk."

Nate had similar thoughts. "I looked through her cell phone and there were only a couple of contacts in it. I didn't bother calling either of them since I couldn't tell whether any of them were family or friends in town."

"You sure you want to get wrapped up in this woman again? She already screwed you once. Why give her the chance to do it again?"

"I'm not getting wrapped up into anything. All I did was stop her from leaving with some random guy and give her a place to lay her head. That's all."

Nate wanted to believe his own words, but deep down inside, he knew it was already too late. On the ride to his house, he kept stealing glances at her in the passenger seat. Liberty was a gorgeous woman who once was full of life. During the ride, he recalled how close they used to be and how much he had missed her. Seeing her again brought all the old feelings, good and bad, back.

"Tammy pointed out that Liberty ran out of J & S twice with red eyes. That doesn't sound like your usual MO, my brotha. Maybe you're losing your touch," Nick cracked.

"Maybe." Neither encounter with Liberty since her return had been normal. What worried Nate most was that she still had a strong effect on him. For years he'd been successful at keeping women at a distance, but Liberty had been back a few days and already his protective instincts had kicked in where she was concerned.

"I'm not sure what's going on with her, but based on our…conversation earlier," he said for a lack of a better way to describe her breakdown, "she's had some rough years."

"What happened to her?"

"I'm not totally sure, but I plan to find out."

Once he ended the call, Nate slid the chair back and pulled a lock box from the bottom desk drawer. Unlocking the metal case and moving some of the important documents aside, his gaze landed on the black velvet box that used to taunt him.

When he flipped open the jewelry box, his pulse amped up as memories rushed through his mind. The simple one carat diamond solitaire twinkled under the office light. Nate still remembered the day he had purchased the ring. It hadn't been exactly what he'd wanted to get, but at the time it had been all he could afford. He hadn't thought about the piece of jewelry in years.

He sat back in the seat still staring at the ring. At the time of purchase, he and Liberty had only known each other for four months. Their connection had been immediate, like nothing he had ever experienced with a woman. He just knew she was the one for him. They had discussed plans for after graduation only weeks before, but during exams and the days leading up to his graduation, they hadn't seen much of each other. A text message here and there was at times their only communication.

So many plans.

Nate had been accepted into Xavier University for grad school, and he and Liberty had planned to have a long-distance relationship until after she graduated. She'd had one more year before completing her undergrad. After that, she intended to go to law school.

With them both having their own set of goals, Liberty didn't think they could maintain their relationship, especially long distance. That was why Nate had planned to propose to her before he graduated from Northwestern. He wanted to prove to her that he had been serious about their relationship and about them being together forever.

But he never got the chance to propose. Never got the chance to recite the speech he had spent endless hours to perfect.

I love you, Nate, but I married Isaac yesterday.

Those words still haunted him. How could she love him, but marry someone else?

Nate slammed the box shut and clutched it within his hand, trying not to hurl it across the room. His gut churned just thinking about how she had betrayed him. But even remembering the pain she had caused, Nate still couldn't stop thinking about her meltdown earlier.

"What did Isaac do to her?"

Nate returned the ring to the metal box, locked it and shoved the container into the drawer. He hadn't done a Google search on Isaac and the Culpepper family since weeks after graduation, but tonight was as good of time as ever.

Isaac had come from old money and Nate could understand why Liberty might have left him for the guy. Culpepper could give her the fairytale lifestyle that Nate hadn't been able to offer at the time. If her breakdown was any indication, life hadn't been as glamorous as either of them thought it would be.

Typing her maiden name into the computer, nothing on her came up. Nate tried Isaac Culpepper. As expected, there were a number of articles on him and his family. Nate didn't give a damn about his family. All he wanted was information about Kayla.

"No, not Kayla, Liberty," he grumbled into the quietness of his office. Scrolling down the list of hits, he stopped.

Trouble in Paradise for the Culpepper Heir

Nate's chest tightened and he clinched his hands into fists when he saw a photo of Isaac and Liberty. The sadness in her eyes was almost his undoing. She had always seemed to carry the weight of the world on her shoulders, but the haunted look in her gaze said something different.

Nate quickly scanned the article which had been published six years earlier. According to the reporter, the couple had been married for seven years at the time. They'd been attending a charity event, and the photographer had caught them in a fiery argument.

Nate studied the photo carefully not liking the way Isaac was gripping her arm, as if trying to keep her from walking away. The long evening gown Liberty wore draped over her slim, but curvy body like it had been made especially for her. Diamonds dripped from her ear lobes and around her neck. She might've looked absolutely stunning in the navy-blue dress, but she was clearly unhappy.

Continuing to peruse the article, Nate's irritation turned into disbelief.

Liberty on drugs? No way. There was no way in hell she'd use drugs, at least not intentionally. Would she? Nate had noticed some changes in her, but...

My life has been a living hell. Her words rattled through his mind as he continued reading. *Drunken stupor. Drugs. Three days missing.*

Nate rubbed his hand over his mouth, deep in thought. He didn't believe half the things written in an article, but what if it had been true? That would explain her drunkenness tonight, but could she have changed that much?

Nate kept reading and skimmed an article that announced they were divorcing. After being married to a multi-millionaire, shouldn't she have received a nice settlement in the divorce to where she didn't have to work?

Liberty's words from their first encounter came rushing back.

Please don't do this, she had said.

Why had she seemed so desperate? Was her new job riding on the proposal?

Reading article after article, and seeing more disturbing photos of Liberty, he grew even more concerned. They needed to talk.

Nate shook his head. "No. She is none of my business. She is none of my business," he repeated over and over. Saying the words out loud did nothing to slow his racing mind. She might not be his business, but…

Liberty had some explaining to do.

Chapter Eight

Liberty opened her eyes slowly, her gaze taking in all she could see without having to turn her head. She couldn't move even if she wanted to. The stiffness in her body was nothing compared to the feel of a college band marching inside her skull. If that wasn't bad enough, the saliva in her mouth had dried up like a Nevada desert.

I will never drink again.

Liberty slowly shifted onto her back. Glancing around the room even with her eyes barely open, it was easy to see that nothing looked familiar.

Fear crept through her body and she bolted upright, only to fall over holding her head.

"Dear, God. Just take me now," she moaned, hoping the pain would subside. "What have I done?"

Bar.

Drinks.

Bruce.

Liberty's heart rate doubled as panic consumed her. She searched her mind trying to put the pieces together of what took place. Had she really seen Nate last night or had it all been a dream?

"Good, you're awake."

Liberty startled at the sound of the familiar voice. So, she hadn't dreamt him. She had actually heard him the night before.

"I guess I don't have to ask how you're feeling."

The bed dipped when he sat next to her and Liberty met his gaze that was filled with concern. Her body heated with his nearness. Even hungover, that magnetic pull she always felt with him was stronger than ever.

After a long hesitation she said, "Hi." The deep, raspiness of her voice sounded unfamiliar.

"Hi yourself." Nate held up a small bottle of aspirin and a glass of water. "I have a feeling you can use these."

He handed her two capsules, and helped with the water when her hands started shaking. She quickly swallowed the pills.

I'll never drink again.

"Do you remember anything about last night?"

Lying against the comfortable pillow, she closed her eyes again and huffed. "The parts I remember I'm trying to forget." She quickly closed her mouth. If the awful taste was any indication, her breath must have been horrid, but Nate didn't seem to notice.

He chuckled. He actually chuckled. Liberty's heart did a flip-flop inside her chest. The arctic freeze treatment he'd given her the last two times they were together had noticeably thawed. Actually, it had started melting before she left his office the day before, but Liberty was too afraid to hope the years apart had been forgotten. No, she planned to keep her guard up in case the *other* Nate that had made an appearance a couple of days ago returned.

"Well, if you haven't figured it out yet, you're at my place. You're welcome to stay as long as you need to. I'll have some breakfast for you whenever you come downstairs."

That last statement sent warmth spreading through her body. Maybe the real Nate was making an appearance. In college, he was one of the most thoughtful people she'd ever met. They were so young, but even at that age, he seemed worldly and mature beyond his years. Charming with a witty sense of humor, good looks and brains, she had fallen for him immediately.

Liberty felt his gaze on her, but didn't look his way. How could she? This was the second time she had embarrassed herself in front of him in only a few days. And not knowing all that happened the night before left her at a disadvantage.

She released an exhausted sigh and took in her surroundings. The large room was decorated with a brown and white color pallet and was very masculine. The bed, with a leather headboard, took up much of the space, but the room still had space for a comfortable chair and table near the bathroom.

It wasn't until the mattress shifted beneath her, signaling Nate had stood, did Liberty chance a glance at him.

"I put a new toothbrush, toothpaste, and towels on the counter in the bathroom. You should find everything else you need in there as well. Come on downstairs when you're ready. I'll make some coffee." He flashed his sexy smile before heading out of the room.

"Nate," Liberty called after he cleared the threshold. He stopped and peeked into the room.

"Yeah?"

"Thank you."

He mumbled something she couldn't quite make out before leaving.

Liberty turned onto her side and faced the window. The blinds were closed, but a sliver of light crept in from the sides of the slats. If she had a dollar for each time she made a bad choice, she'd be rich. When was she going to get her life together? She was smart, a hard worker, and resilient. Why did she always end up doing something stupid like getting drunk, only to snap her into reality this morning?

Thirty minutes later, the smell of coffee permeated the air and Liberty stepped out of the bedroom. She had freshened up, but was too tired to care that her clothes were wrinkled, or that she had to finger comb her hair into submission. Walking around without wearing any makeup made her uncomfortable, but she couldn't continue hiding out in the bedroom. Tempting though it was to relax in Nate's guest bed, she knew at some point she would have to face him.

Liberty headed for the stairs, her bare feet quiet against the plush carpet. Moving down the long hallway she passed two bedrooms and a bathroom before getting to the stairwell. At the opposite end was another room that she assumed was the master bedroom.

"Nate?" Liberty called out when she reached the main floor. The house was bigger than she had first thought. In addition to the rooms upstairs, there was an office, formal dining room and a living room from what she could see.

"I'm in the kitchen. Turn right at the bottom of the stairs."

Liberty followed his voice and the banging of pots and pans down a short hallway. The delicious smell of food filling the air, made her hungrier, but not even the promise of food and coffee could calm her pounding heart. Talk about the walk of shame. How would she explain her behavior from the night before?

Might as well get this over with.

Liberty slowed as she walked by one piece of artwork after another lining the walls. The vibrant colors and intricate designs leaped off the canvas. Each piece more spectacular than the next.

"My cousin Christina painted those," Nate said from the kitchen entrance, a dishtowel in his hands.

"They're amazing. Is she a professional artist or is this something she does in her spare time?"

"As much as she charged me, she'd better be a professional."

Liberty smiled and followed Nate into the kitchen. She took in the large space, that held a small dinette set off to the side and a breakfast bar that overlooked a family room.

"Have a seat." He nodded his head toward the long breakfast bar.

Easing onto the bar stool, Liberty continued surveying her surroundings. The bright walls were a nice contrast to the dark floors and cabinets. Modern appliances rounded out the contemporary kitchen.

She glanced behind her and immediately fell in love with the family room. The dark gray walls, the floor to ceiling brick fireplace, and the oversized leather furniture looked inviting. But it was the wood ceiling panels with dark beams stretching the length of the room that really caught her attention. Instead of the sofa facing the fireplace, it faced the wall of glass on the opposite side of the room that provided a ton of natural light. The view outside included a deck that overlooked a moderate size yard.

"I hope you're hungry."

Liberty turned back to the kitchen and her stomach chose that moment to rumble, sending heat rushing to her cheeks.

Nate flashed a knowing smile. "I'll take that as a yes. I wasn't sure what you had a taste for, but I made a little bit of everything. Do you still take your coffee black with two sugars?"

"I can't believe you remember." Sorrow pierced her heart. She'd been married to her ex-husband for almost thirteen years and he could barely remember her birthday.

"I remember everything about you," Nate said, setting a large mug in front of her.

His gorgeous brown eyes met hers and the heat that originally started in her cheeks spread throughout the rest of her body. How could one look, after so many years apart, make her still feel all tingly inside? The man had an effect on her that she couldn't deny and he looked so good. Like each time she'd seen him, his mustache and goatee were perfectly groomed. Whether he was suited up or dressed casually, he made anything he wore look outrageously sexy. Even now, the way the blue T-shirt he had on stretched across his wide chest and molded around his muscular biceps had her mouth watering.

Nate cleared his throat, effectively breaking the temporary trance that she had fallen into. He cast her one last glance and swallowed hard before moving back to the stove. Maybe she wasn't the only one impacted.

Liberty shook the thought free. No way he could be feeling what she was feeling. She looked a mess in her rumpled clothes, disheveled hair, and bare face.

The steam from her coffee billowed above the rim and she took a tentative sip of the dark liquid. Nate moved around the kitchen effortlessly. By the looks of the high-end appliances, fully stocked kitchen, and the way he wielded a knife, it was safe to say he spent a lot of time in the space.

How different would her life had been had she chosen the right man? Someone to come home to, who would actually be there. Someone who cared enough to listen to what she had to say. Someone who cooked for her.

"Let's talk about last night." Nate interrupted her thoughts. "I assume you didn't know the man you were about to leave the bar with."

Liberty felt like the stupidest woman on the face of the earth. She hadn't eaten and then drank too much. The bits and pieces leading up to this catastrophe of the night before made her want to puke. What had she been thinking? Actually, she hadn't been thinking. Going to the bar was an escape from her reality. Embarrassing herself by falling apart in Nate's office, on top of all the stress she'd been under, had triggered her need to let loose.

Liberty looked up. The burning intensity of Nate's gaze met hers, probably waiting for her to respond.

"No. I didn't know him. Besides you, the only people I know in town are my sister, her fiancé and a few co-workers, though I don't know them well."

"Then why the hell were you leaving with the man, Liberty?" Nate snapped and then shook his head and cursed under his breath. "Sorry. It's just that anything could have happened to you last night. I'm trying not to think about what that guy could have done to you."

Liberty's heart shifted in her chest at the angst in his tone. It had been so long since anyone, other than Demi, gave a crap about her well-being. Of all the people to show interest now, she never would have pegged Nate to be that person.

"I—I needed an escape," she finally said honestly. "Going to the bar seemed like a good idea at the time. Please don't think that's my norm, Nate." Even if they weren't a couple, she didn't want him to think the worst about her. "I have a glass of wine on special occasions, but I have never been drunk. I'm not a drinker."

"You've *never* been drunk?" he asked, disbelief ringing in his tone.

"Never."

An unreadable look flashed across his face, but instead of saying anything, he placed several dishes on the counter in front of her. She took in the stack of pancakes, eggs, hash browns, fruit, sausages and bacon. Even though she wasn't a meat eater, everything looked good. As for the eggs, though she had incorporated them back into her diet, they still made her gag sometimes.

"This is a lot of food."

"Just eat what you want and I'll take care of the rest, but considering how much you drank last night, you might want to eat it all."

There had been something in his gaze a moment ago that made her uneasy. Did he really not believe her?

"I know you don't trust me, but I'm telling you the truth. What you saw last night was a one-time thing. I'm never getting drunk again."

He sat next to her and after a short hesitation he said, "I believe you, but I'm a little confused."

"By what?"

He piled breakfast items onto his plate, and Liberty remembered how much he liked to eat. Considering he didn't have a lick of fat on him, she had no idea where he stored the food.

She added a pancake, and a little watermelon and cantaloupe to her plate while waiting for Nate to respond. She wondered if her stomach could handle this little bit.

"I realized yesterday in my office that there's so much I don't know about you. Since I still have questions, I started by Googling you last night."

"You Googled me? Why?" The volume of her voice rose with each word. Disappointment clawed through her that he had resorted to looking her up online.

His fork stopped midway to his mouth. "What else was I supposed to do? You didn't want to discuss the past. Then you had a meltdown in my office. Last night I watched you try to drink your problems away, and if that wasn't bad enough, you almost left the bar with some asshole. Since you were in no condition to shed light on what was going on with you, I started with the internet."

"What do you want to ask me, Nate?" She had already decided to answer any questions he had. That was the least she could do.

"Why the name change?"

Of all that he could have asked, she hadn't expected that question first.

"Years ago, when I threatened to leave Isaac, he leaked lies about me to the media. He and his family are well connected in Chicago. During the divorce, he blackballed me around town to many of his business associates. I had been a paralegal, as well as a project manager at his family's law firm. After leaving there, finding a decent job had been impossible. I wanted to start over, change my identity, and separate myself from him and his family in every way possible."

"Of all the names you could have picked, why Liberty?" Nate asked.

"Because of the meaning. Living in Isaac's world was oppressive, and had stripped me of my independence, self-esteem and anything else I could claim as my own. I wanted my power back." Her words had more bite than intended as she pushed down the disgust she felt for Isaac and the disappointment she had in herself for giving him her power in the first place. "Liberty means the condition of being free within society from oppressive restrictions. Choosing that name was my own form of…of rebellion, I guess. I needed to take back the control I had given away."

Nate nodded, as if satisfied with her response.

"When did you stop eating sausage?" he asked, taking the conversation in a different direction as he pointed to the plate of sausage patties. "There was a time when you would have eaten all of those, as well as the ones on my plate."

Liberty laughed, something she hadn't done often enough lately. There was a time she'd eat anything put in front of her, especially meat. "I'm a vegetarian now."

The left side of his luscious lips tilted and that sexy mouth curled into a heart-stopping grin. Lust shot through her system and that thrill she used to experience back when they were dating was in full bloom. Everything about the man was *hot*.

"Now *that's* a shock." He laughed and she joined in. Her new way of eating had started over five years ago when she realized how much meat she consumed. She gave it up for a month and soon noticed how much better she felt physically.

Once they were finished eating, Nate went to the coffee pot and brought the carafe over to refill their mugs. The headache that Liberty had awakened with was now a dull ache. She didn't know what had helped, the aspirin, coffee or the delicious meal.

"Come on. Grab your cup and let's go to the family room."

They sat on the sofa, and Nate set his mug on the cocktail table in front of them. After taking a sip of her drink, she placed her cup down.

"Your home is lovely. Did you decorate it yourself?" What she'd seen of the house, the décor fit Nate's personality perfectly. At least from what she could recall of him. The person she experienced in his office the day before wasn't who she remembered. But the man who had come to her rescue last night and treated her with kindness today was the man she had fallen in love with.

Nate chuckled. "Not hardly. There are too many women in my family who enjoy spending other people's money and decorating homes. Most of the bachelors in our family have learned to come up with a budget, and get one of our aunts or cousins to fix our places up. My cousin Christina, who oversees the painting department at J & S, took care of the color scheme and painting. And Martina, she's the big mouth who barged in on us yesterday, not only works in the office with me and Nick, but she's a carpenter by trade. She remodeled the kitchen, added the built-ins." He nodded toward the shelving units on either side of the fireplace. "And she built my back deck. My cousin Jada, the fashionista of the family, dragged me to every furniture store in Ohio. I may never move from this house just so I don't have to relive the whole decorating experience."

Liberty smiled, still looking around at his home from where she sat. "Well, they did an amazing job. Everything is so comfortable and inviting."

Nate studied her before saying, "I'm glad you think so." His deep, intoxicating voice sent a wave of something she couldn't identify through her body. And the way he was looking at her…memories of what they once shared came crashing back with a force.

How had she chosen so wrong?

Liberty shook the thought free. Back then, helping her family was all she knew to do. She had chosen to be responsible and ended up sacrificing the love of a lifetime. She had chosen financial security over happiness. She had chosen Isaac over Nate.

The biggest mistake of my life.

"Why did you leave me?" Nate asked as if reading her mind. "Why did you throw away what we had for that asshole, Isaac?"

Chapter Nine

Nate hadn't planned to start the conversation like that, but his patience had run out. If he was ever going to get over her betrayal, he needed her to explain to him what went wrong.

"I need you to know something. Something I should have made very clear before walking away from you that day," Liberty said, moving closer to him.

There had been a lot she should've told him before that day, but Nate didn't bother pointing that out.

"I never slept with Isaac when you and I were together. I rarely even saw him."

"Then how the hell did you end up marrying the guy, Liberty? The not knowing how you could have fallen in love with another man while you and I were together is what's bugged me the most."

"I *never* loved him. Never," she said with conviction. "I only really saw him when he came into the restaurant where I was working. We didn't spend time together and he knew you and I were seeing each other. Every now and then he'd be outside of my dorm when I left for class or work. It was always a quick hi and bye. But… At the time, I felt like I had to marry him."

She and Isaac had dated off and on during her freshmen and sophomore year of college. She hadn't talked much about him, but Nate knew he was two years older, had a job waiting for him after graduating, and drove a brand-new Corvette. Nate hadn't been intimidated by the guy, but he never thought Liberty the type to be swayed by material things.

Irritation gnawed at him. Suddenly he wasn't sure he could sit through hearing about her and Isaac's life together.

"This whole situation started with my family. My mother was diagnosed with sickle cell disease as a child, and had mild problems growing up," Liberty said. "She didn't really start having complications until after I was born. Even more so when she got pregnant with my sister, Demi."

Nate listened intently, curious to understand what her family had to do with any of this. Liberty explained how her mother on occasion had a crisis when some of her blood cells became blocked causing severe pain. Doctors had been able to control the pain to a point, but her mother had spent a lot of time in and out of the hospital. All the while hospital bills continued to grow.

"Did you inherit the disease?" Nate asked. She had never been sick while they dated, except once when she had the flu.

"No. I didn't, but my sister has the trait."

Nate released a sigh of relief, not realizing he'd been holding his breath. He and Liberty weren't a couple, and technically her health wasn't any of his business. Yet, that concern he felt for her the night before hadn't subsided.

She fidgeted in her seat. Nibbling on her lower lip as if trying not to get emotional. "During each episode, my father refused to leave her side. Unfortunately, that meant he had a hard time holding onto jobs. With only a high school education, he barely made minimum wage. We were already living below poverty and their financial situation grew worse."

Liberty stood. She walked across the room and gazed out the window. Seconds ticked by before she returned her attention to him.

"My sister called a few days before your graduation, telling me they'd been evicted. The three of them were living in a homeless shelter." She stopped again, shaking her head. "My father was too proud to keep asking his family for help. Especially when they couldn't understand why he took off of work whenever my mother was in the hospital." Liberty's voice cracked and she cleared her throat and took a few breaths.

Nate realized he hadn't known her as well as he thought he had. They'd been so young and in love that nothing or no one else seemed to matter. Like most college students, neither of them had much money, but he had no idea her situation had been so oppressive.

"I felt so helpless. I was already sending home practically everything I made at my part-time job. It never seemed to be enough. The hospital bills were outrageous. I considered dropping out of school to get a full-time job, but I had one more year of school and was on a full scholarship."

"Where was I when you got this call? Why didn't I know about any of this?"

"I was finishing up a shift at work. Between me working, taking exams, and you getting ready for graduation, we hadn't seen much of each other those last couple of weeks of school."

"But we talked or texted every day." Nate went to her, seeing how agitated she was getting as she rubbed her hands together, unable to stand still. Despite a sudden desire to comfort her, he stopped a few feet away to keep from pulling her into his arms. They needed to hash this out once and for all and touching her might bring an end to the conversation. "I don't understand why you didn't tell me any of this. I could've helped."

"I was embarrassed, Nate. I never told you I was poor because it wasn't something I wanted people to know. At Northwestern, I was surrounded by students who seemed rich compared to me. I didn't want anyone looking down on me or treating me differently."

Nate knew she hadn't had much money by her clothes. She didn't have many and most looked as if she'd had them awhile. But he hadn't cared. He fell in love with her kindness and compassion for others, and how special she made him feel.

"How does Isaac fit into all of this?"

Liberty fidgeted with the sleeve of her blouse, and swallowed hard before looking at him. "Isaac showed up in the parking lot of the restaurant while I was on the phone with Demi."

"How convenient," Nate grumbled and turned away, running his hand over his hair and down to the back of his neck.

"You have to understand. He caught me at a time when I was at a loss for what to do. He already knew some of my history and my family's struggles from when we dated. He had often talked about us getting married and becoming a power couple like his parents. I'll admit, back then I did fantasize about what it would be like not to worry about money.

"The night of the phone call, he drove me to my apartment. He told me there's no reason my parents or I needed to struggle financially. That he could help with everything, including getting them into a house, getting my father a flexible job, taking care of hospital bills, and setting up a college fund for my sister. That's when he came up with the idea that we get married."

Nate narrowed his eyes. "You honestly believe that he just happened to come up with that idea on a fly? If you didn't love him, I'm assuming this was a marriage of convenience and you had to sign something."

She nodded. "I had to sign a contract."

"When did he give you the document to sign?"

Liberty glanced down at her hands. "The next morning."

Nate paced the length of the room, wanting to throw something at the wall, and too pissed to listen to any more. Before they had started dating exclusively, Liberty had told him that she broke things off with Isaac because he had a mean streak. Yet, she ended up marrying the guy anyway.

"You know what? I can't do this. I thought I wanted to know, but—"

"I know hearing all of this is awful, but it's not easy for me to tell you how gullible and insecure I was back then, Nate. So that we can move on and put this behind us, I want you to understand where my head was at then. I was twenty, my family was in trouble, and Isaac, who was wealthy, presented a way for me to help them. Unless you've lived in poverty for any period of time, you'll *never* truly understand what that meant to someone like me."

Nate reclaimed his seat on the sofa and reached for his mug. Right now, he needed something a hell of a lot stronger than coffee. Liberty reclaimed her seat, but kept some distance between them.

For the next hour, she talked more about her family instead of Isaac. She must have sensed that, though he was curious about her marriage to Isaac and what she had endured with him, he didn't want to hear about it right now.

He hated that this all could have been cleared up had they known each other better, and discussed their families more. Had he known hers was in dire straits, he would have done everything in his power to help them.

Some of Nate's anger for the way she had handled the situation then had subsided, and the longer they sat talking the more he was reminded of what had attracted him to her in the first place. She had a gentle spirit and a soft heart for people. He had recognized those qualities in college when she used to do volunteer work. He had often wondered how she fit it all in. Her class load hadn't been easy and she had often sacrificed parties and weekend trips for studying.

"My mother often commented that my dad was her best friend," Liberty said absently as she fiddled with her shirt sleeve. "I remember one instance when I was a sophomore in high school and my mother had spent a week in the hospital. The first night she was back home, I was helping her get ready for bed and she told me to make sure that when I get married, to marry someone who loved me more than they loved themselves."

Liberty's teary-eyed gaze met his.

"I know before you graduated we had talked about trying a long-distance relationship. Though I wanted to believe that you wouldn't forget me once you left Chicago, I honestly didn't know if you would come back for me once I graduated. I loved you so much, Nate, and I felt your love for me, but I forfeited love for financial security. In doing so, I made such a mess of my life thinking I was doing the right thing."

Nate leaned forward, his elbows on his thighs and sighed. His grandmother often said, *no use living with regret. Everything happens for a reason.*

"Where are your parents now?" Nate asked.

"They passed away a few years ago. My mother died from a stroke and two days later, my dad died."

"Aww, baby, I'm sorry." Nate covered her hand and squeezed. That familiar zing he felt whenever they touched was just as strong as usual.

"Thank you. My parents were so close. It was as if their hearts were beating as one. I didn't know how my father was going to survive without her." She shrugged. "Turns out he didn't."

Nate continued holding Liberty's hand. He would never ever complain about his own life again. He couldn't imagine losing one of his parents, let alone both of them at the same time. And though his parents weren't wealthy, they had given him and Nick the best of everything. Nate didn't know what it was like to go without a meal or not live in a nice home.

"I don't know what to say."

"You don't have to say anything. Thanks for listening."

"I wished you had told me what was going on at home while we were dating. I could've helped, Liberty. My family would've helped."

"I didn't know that, Nate. I'm not proud of my decisions, but I was young and did the best I could. The day I left home, my dad told me that people like us didn't often get scholarships from places like Northwestern. That I had to grab hold of every opportunity and make something of myself. I was concerned about them, but he told me not to worry about home. They'd be okay. So when I left for Chicago, I tried to pretend I was someone else. I didn't want to be that poor, black girl from the rough side of Columbus."

Nate understood that more than she knew. It was the main reason he had gone by Moore instead of Jenkins-Moore in college. In Cincinnati, the Jenkins family seemed to be known by everyone. Given the chance to attend college out of state had been a godsend. He wanted to be his own person and not continue walking in the shadow of his uncles or cousins.

"Maybe one day I'll tell you more about the last thirteen years. I haven't talked to anyone about me and Isaac, except now my sister knows a little of what went on. As part of the contract I had with Isaac, I agreed to stay married a minimum of twenty years and I couldn't say anything about what we agreed to that night. Not even to my parents. I basically sold my soul to the devil."

"Wait," Nate said confused. "It's only been thirteen years. What did the agreement say about you leaving the marriage early?"

Liberty glanced away. "I walked away with what I went into the marriage with, which was nothing."

Watching her fidget with a loose thread at the bottom of her shirt, he wondered what she wasn't telling him.

"What happened? Why'd you break the contract?"

Liberty pulled her bottom lip between her teeth and rubbed her forehead nervously. "I—I couldn't stay married to him any longer. I should've left years ago, but when he..." Her voice shook, but she maintained her composure.

"When he what?" Nate asked cautiously, a tight knot twisting his gut, fearing what she would say.

"He—he hit me. He broke my jaw one night when I refused to sleep with him."

Nate's fists clenched at his sides. The thought of any man hitting a woman, for any reason, disgusted him. But knowing Isaac had put his hands on her made Nate want to hunt him down and beat his ass.

Nate bolted off the sofa and went back to pacing, unable to sit while trying to get his emotions under control.

"After that I couldn't stay," she said.

"Of course, you couldn't stay! You shouldn't have married the ruthless bastard in the first place!"

Liberty stiffened, but remained in her seat.

Damn. He hadn't intended to say that, but he couldn't hold the thought in. "I'm sorry. I know it's none of my—"

"You don't have to apologize. You're right. I shouldn't have married a man like him and a man I didn't love, but…" She shrugged, looking worn out.

Nate hadn't liked Isaac the first time they'd met and right now, he hated the man's guts. Liberty had had a promising future while in college. Had she accomplished any of the goals she'd set for herself? Had she gotten her law degree?

A quick glance at her sitting on the sofa, her head back and eyes closed told him those were questions for another day.

"Why don't we table the rest of this conversation for now. You look like you're about to pass out."

She sat forward and smile, but it didn't reach her eyes. "I'm all right, but yeah, I think I've said enough. I'm sure this is not how you planned to spend a Saturday morning, and thank you for last night. I…" Her mouth clamped shut and she blushed at her words. "I mean…I didn't mean it like it sounded."

Nate chuckled and reached for her hand. "I know what you meant."

He pulled her up from the sofa and into his arms. Needing to hold her if only for a moment. Her soft, curvy body molded against him and when she shivered, he held her tighter. If only he could have protected her from what she'd gone through.

They stood that way, in the middle of his family room, for the longest time, until Nate eventually released her. "I know that I keep apologizing for my behavior, but I really am sorry. The thought that you might've ended up at the bar last night because of my jacked-up attitude makes me sick. I honestly didn't mean to hurt you yesterday."

"Yes, you did." She smiled when his mouth fell open in surprise. "But I understand. If I were in your shoes, I would've behaved the same way. I hurt you and for that, I'm truly sorry. Nate, walking away from you was the hardest thing I've ever had to do. If I could have a do over, I'd take it in a heartbeat, but I know life doesn't work that way. At least not my life. I'm such a screw up. I—"

"Stop." Nate moved closer. So close that if he lowered his head, his lips could easily touch hers and he shuddered at the thought. The way she was staring at his mouth, he wondered if she was thinking the same thing.

"I hate hearing you talk down on yourself." He cupped her cheek and she leaned into his touch, staring into his eyes. "You were young. We were young. Maybe your life wasn't perfect, but you survived. I really admire that you're working to get your life back on track. I know it can't be easy, but if there's anything I can do to help, let me know."

"You have no idea how much you saying that means to me." Her eyes filled with tears, but she blinked them back. "It's…it's been a long time since someone, outside of my sister, offered to help me in any way."

He nodded and dropped his hand, taking a step back to stop himself from acting on the desire to see if her lips were as soft as he remembered.

"I'll help you clean up the kitchen." She hurried away from him and started clearing the breakfast bar. "Then I should be heading home."

"Stop." He took the plates from her and set them in the sink. "I can take care of this later. Besides, I brought you here. I'll drop you off wherever you want to go."

"*Oh crap.* I forgot I didn't have my car."

"Where is it?"

"It's in the shop. It broke down on me yesterday after I left your office."

Nate shook his head. "Talk about shitty days."

"If only you knew," she mumbled under her breath, but Nate heard her.

He had vowed never to forgive this woman for what she'd done to him, to them. But now he had an overwhelming desire to get to know Liberty Stewart.

Chapter Ten

A short while later, Nate backed his late model BMW out of the two-car attached garage with Liberty sitting in the passenger seat. Since she'd been asleep when arriving at his place, she took in the quiet neighborhood with the tree-lined streets.

"What area of town is this?" she asked, settling into the soft leather seat that wrapped cozily around her body.

"Wyoming, which reminds me…" he pulled the car over and lifted his sunglasses to the top of his head, "…where do you live?"

Liberty met his grin and smiled. "I guess that would help, huh?"

She gave him her address and watched as he plugged it into his GPS. Once they were on their way, Liberty sat back in the seat. The last couple of hours had been spent talking and had felt so normal despite the subject matter. Sharing some of her past with Nate had been hard and embarrassing, but so far Liberty hadn't felt any judgment from him like she had expected.

She almost leaped out of her skin when Nate's hand covered hers. The move was so unexpected, Liberty didn't know what to think or say. A blast of desire consumed her and she had to suppress the moan clogging her throat. Did he have any idea what his touched did to her? Could he possibly know how often she had fantasized about what it would feel like to be with him again?

"Relax," was all he said. He didn't explain why he held her hand. He just kept his attention on the road as he brushed his thumb back and forth gently over the top of her hand. Such a simple gesture, but the sweet torture of each stroke made it hard to do as he said—relax.

Liberty exhaled a shuddery breath, trying not to read too much into his kindness. This was who he was. The man she remembered.

The last twenty-four hours had been an emotional roller coaster, but thanks to him, she had weathered the emotional storm. She couldn't remember the last time she'd felt taken care of and was hesitant to admit that she could get used to the feeling.

They rode in silence and the smooth ride of the car, as well as the soft jazz flowing through the speakers lulled her into a relaxed state. Her eyes drifted closed. Why couldn't she feel this way all the time? Calm. At peace. Maybe there was something to sharing secrets and getting *stuff* off your chest. It was as if a weight had been lifted. Granted she and Nate still didn't know much about each other. At least he finally understood what happened and why she had married Isaac.

"Wake-up, sleeping beauty."

Liberty slowly opened her eyes to find Nate's gaze steady on her, and his large hand still holding hers. Not realizing she had dozed off, she blinked several times until the sleep fog dissipated.

She glanced out the window, surprised to see that they were sitting in front of her apartment building. The eight-unit structure that needed a paint job, new windows, and had a less than manicured lawn was a far cry from the area they'd just left. Though the complex was advertised as secure, a brick—that was often used—held open the door. Two older women, one fixing the clothes on a toddler and one smoking, sat on the front stoop while a few children ran around chasing each other and trampling the grass.

What did Nate think about her living here? If his snappy clothes, his gorgeous home and automobiles were any indication, he was accustomed to the finer things of life.

Nate squeezed her hand before releasing it, and then slipped his dark shades over his eyes. The man was already too sexy for his own good, and the sunglasses only emphasized that fact. "Ready to go in?" he asked.

"Oh…yeah." Liberty undid her seatbelt while Nate climbed out of the car and strolled around to the passenger door. When he opened it, he extended his hand to help her out. "Thank you."

"My pleasure."

Still a gentleman. Liberty recognized a few changes in him since college, but the way he treated her, like she was special, hadn't changed at all. He was still a sweetheart.

"Thanks for the ride," she said as they stood next to the car. "And I really appreciate you coming to my rescue last night."

"Stop thanking me. I'm glad I was there. Just promise me one thing."

Nate boldly slid his arm around her waist, and Liberty tried to remain calm and not hyperventilate at the excitement fluttering in her stomach. His fresh scent teased her while his hard body pressed against hers, sending her senses into overdrive. Hell, she was about ready to promise him anything he wanted.

"Think twice about going to bars alone." He spoke quietly against her ear and his warm breath let loose a swarm of butterflies within her. "If you want to go out and drink, call me. I'll go with you. If you would prefer not to go with me, then get your sister to tag along with you. Because the thought of you putting yourself in harm's way bothers me."

Liberty couldn't see his eyes, but felt his intense gaze on her. All she could do was nod her agreement since she didn't trust her voice. This whole getting up close and personal thing he had going on, while whispering in her ear and showing concern for her well-being, had her heart skipping at least three beats.

"As for you drinking—"

"I won't. I'm never drinking alcohol again," she promised, meaning every word.

His enticing lips, which she longed to kiss, twitched as if fighting a smile. "Baby, I'm not suggesting you give up drin—"

"You don't have to. I've learned my lesson." It had taken the whole morning to get the pounding headache down to a slight throb. "I won't be getting drunk or putting myself in the predicament I was in last night. But thanks for being willing to go to the bar with me if needed."

He chuckled. "Anytime. Now, let's get you inside."

"Nate, you don't have to walk—"

"I want to. Let's go," he said, his hand at the small of her back guiding her forward and sending a wave of lust shooting through her body. It was hard enough being close to him again, but each time he touched her, heat set her nerve endings on fire.

He stayed close as they strolled up the walkway. Liberty nodded a hello and flashed a small smile to the women sitting near the door, but they only had eyes for Nate. Their gazes checked him out from the top of his head down to the white Nikes on his feet. But who could blame them? The man was a walking billboard for everything tall, dark, and sexy as hell, especially with the sun glasses on.

Nate greeted the women with a slight nod, but didn't stop moving and followed Liberty inside. They walked up one flight of stairs before reaching her apartment.

"Would you like to come in?" she asked, sticking the key into the lock.

"Sure."

She pushed the door open and took a cursory look around, glad the place was neat. The apartment came furnished and was easy to keep clean since she didn't have a lot of personal items.

"Make yourself comfortable." She turned on the old-model, 19-inch television more out of habit than her desire to watch TV. Living alone, she preferred having a little background noise even though the volume was usually low. "Can I get you something to drink? I have water and apple juice."

"Apple juice sounds good," Nate said absently as he stared out the single window in the living room. She didn't have a view, unless he considered a brick wall and an alley something to look at. There was a time she might've been embarrassed by her meager living space, but the struggle she endured after the divorce was a humbling experience. Now she was grateful for everything she had, including her tiny apartment.

If her home was below Nate's standards, he didn't show it. He roamed around, taking it all in, but said nothing.

Liberty walked over and handed him the glass of apple juice. She placed her glass of water on a coaster on the cocktail table in front of the love seat before sitting.

"We've discussed me and some of the drama that was my life, tell me about you. Why go by Moore instead of Jenkins-Moore?"

Nate smiled and sipped his juice, but didn't sit down. Instead, he leaned his shoulder against a nearby wall and crossed his legs at the ankles. Liberty wondered if their closeness outside shook him the way it had shaken her. She was okay with him being on the other side of the room. The distance gave her heart a chance to settle down.

"When Nick and I were growing up, kids used to ask us why we had two last names all the time. It didn't bother Nick, but for some reason it bugged the heck out of me. I didn't want to be different. Most kids had one last name and that's what I wanted."

"I'm surprised it was a big deal to you."

Nate shrugged. "Looking back, I'm surprised too. When I was in middle school, my mother told me that if it bothered me that much, once I turn eighteen I could change my name. I had planned to drop Jenkins and just keep Moore. But by then, I had grown to appreciate what the Jenkins name and family meant to me. So, I kept it hyphenated."

"Why didn't you talk about your family much in college?" she asked.

Nick hesitated and stared into his glass of juice. "For years, I went through life in the shadow of the Jenkins name," Nate finally said. "When I left for college, I had immediately decided that I was going to go by my dad's last name, Moore. Don't get me wrong. I was proud to carry both names, but the Jenkins family is *huge*. It seemed everyone in Cincinnati knew at least one, and they especially knew my uncles and all of their shenanigans growing up." He chuckled. "When people found out Nick and I were related to the Jenkins clan, it just got to be too much. We attracted good and bad attention. I know this is going to sound crazy, especially since the name is very common, but I felt that by not using the name in college, it gave me a bit of anonymity that I didn't have here. Living here, I couldn't do anything that didn't get back to someone in the family."

A slow smile crept over Liberty's lips. She bet he was adorable when he was little. "Were you a bad kid growing up? Did people report back to your family because you were cutting up?"

Nate grinned and then started laughing. He pushed off the wall and strolled across the room. When he approached the love seat, he stopped and removed the cell phone from his pocket and set it on the table before sitting down. There was a little space between them, but Liberty's body still responded to his closeness.

"Nick was the bad one," Nate finally said. "He didn't care if people reported anything to our family. Even at a young age I didn't want people in my business. You couldn't do anything wrong. Otherwise, my grandparents found out and then my parents. And *then* we'd get one of my grandfather's famous speeches. '*Your actions don't only affect you. They affect the whole family. Everything you say and do is a representation of this family.*'"

Liberty laughed at the way he changed his voice to a deep, gritty tone. "So did it work?"

"Did what work?"

"Did you feel like you were your own person while you were in Chicago?"

Nate nodded. "As a matter of fact, I did. I grew up a lot. It felt good to find my own identity and not be compared to my brother, cousins or uncles. I had a chance to just be me and I liked the person I was."

Liberty smiled. "Me too."

Before either of them could say anything else, Nate's phone vibrated against the tabletop, and he glanced at the screen. "Excuse me for one second."

"Take your time." Liberty stood with her glass and went into the kitchen to give him some space. The small size of her apartment didn't allow for much privacy. Though she could only hear one side of the conversation, she could tell Nate was probably leaving soon when he glanced at his watch.

It was just as well. Getting too comfortable having him around wasn't a good idea. He had a life and just because they were on speaking terms didn't mean that they could ever be more than friends.

Liberty jumped when someone pounded on her door. With her hand over her heart, as if that would slow how fast it was beating, she glanced into the living room. Nate was standing, a frown on his handsome face when the knocking became frantic.

"Hold on, Jerry," Nate said into the phone and then covered the mouth piece. "Are you expecting someone?"

"No, but it's probably my neighbor from across the hall." Yvonne and her husband were an elderly couple that had welcomed Liberty to the building the first day she moved in. They were some of the nicest people she'd met in a long time.

"Check the peep hole before you open the door," Nate said, concern on his face.

"Really, Nate?" She couldn't hold back a smile. "I've been on my own a long time. I've got this." He was overprotective to a fault, still, but she loved him for it.

Nate shrugged and told whoever he'd been talking to that he would call them back, and then was right behind Liberty as she moved to the door.

She confirmed it was indeed Yvonne and swung open the door. "Hey, what's going on."

"Oh, thank God you're…" Yvonne's panicked voice trailed off as she peered over Liberty's shoulder. "I—I'm sorry. I didn't realize you had company."

"It's okay," Liberty touched the woman's arm, noting how hard she was breathing. "What happened? What's wrong?"

"It's my husband. He's fallen again. Can you help me lift him?"

"Of course. Let me get my keys." Liberty tried to move around Nate, but he caught her by the waist.

"I'll help her husband up." Then he turned to Yvonne. "Just show me where he is."

Seeing the concerned look on Yvonne's face, Liberty assured the older woman that it was fine. Nate went ahead and Liberty grabbed her keys and hurried to lock the door. By the time she made it across the hall, Nate had introduced himself and helped Arthur into his favorite chair.

Liberty approached Yvonne and placed her arm around the sobbing woman's shoulders. "Why are you so upset? He looks fine, and he's already back to fussing about the baseball players on TV."

Yvonne shook her head. "I don't know how much longer I'll be able to care for him by myself. Our son thinks it's time we put him in a nursing home and I agree, but

Arthur is fighting it. Saying he can take care of himself. I don't know what to do." The woman sobbed.

Liberty made eye contact with Nate across the room. She couldn't read his expression, but she didn't want to leave Yvonne in this condition. This was the second time Arthur had fallen since Liberty moved in, and according to his wife, it was getting more frequent.

"Here, have a seat. I'll make you a cup of tea," Liberty said to Yvonne and pulled out the chair. She knew where the woman kept everything since she visited Yvonne and Arthur often.

"Did Arthur finally agree to go to the doctor?" Liberty asked quietly.

"Yes. He has an appointment Tuesday. Hopefully, we won't have any more incidents before then."

For the next twenty minutes, she and Yvonne talked and the woman was back to her smiling self. Liberty glanced at Nate again and when he gestured with his head toward the door, Liberty stood.

"Yvonne, I'll be right back."

Nate said his goodbyes to the couple and followed Liberty into the hallway.

"I'm so glad you were here," Liberty whispered the moment he pulled the door closed. "Thank you so much for your help."

"Of course, but Liberty that man is too heavy for either of you to be trying to lift. If he falls again, call 911."

She nodded. "I will."

"I need to get going. Are you going to be all right?" They were standing so close. All Liberty would have to do is lift up on her tip-toes and their mouths would be joined. But she didn't. No way would she do anything that could possibly ruin any progress they'd made to becoming friends again.

"I'll be fine. They both seemed a little shaken, so I'm going to sit with them for another hour or so."

Nate smiled. "I see you're still a softy, but I'm serious when I say don't try to lift Arthur. Call for help if needed all right?"

"And I see you're still overprotective," she said instead of answering him.

He chuckled. "Maybe a little."

She'd been back in his life for less than a week and already he was reminding her of why she had fallen in love with him in the first place. It also made her feel like an idiot all over again for not confiding in him about her family all those years ago.

"Don't worry about me and Yvonne. We'll be fine."

"You always did have a big heart for helping others."

During college Liberty had volunteered every other week at a nursing home, and helped served meals whenever she could at a nearby homeless shelter. Despite what she had gone through growing up, or how worried she'd been about her family while in college, she always reminded herself that there were others who were worse off.

Nate's hand moved to the nape of her neck and pulled her close, his gaze steady on her mouth. When he slowly lowered his head, a streak of excitement tumbled through her. He hadn't even kissed her, yet it was as if she could already feel his delicious mouth on hers. But one look at the uncertainty radiating in his eyes and she reigned in her eagerness.

Instead of Nate's lips touching hers, he placed a lingering kiss against her temple. It might have been an innocent kiss and maybe even a little chaste, but the gesture meant more to her than she could ever express.

He lifted his head but didn't remove his hand from the back of her neck. Worry lines marred his forehead. She had no idea what he was thinking but he seemed conflicted.

Nate dropped his hand and took a step back. "Let's talk Monday so we can identify some days to work on the Unity Tower project." The man she had spent much of the last twenty-four hours with was gone. In his place was the business man who wanted to keep their relationship professional.

For just a little while she had been able to enjoy the man who had once meant the world to her. Oh well, she'd rather have him as a friend than an enemy.

"Okay. Until Monday then."

Chapter Eleven

Nate pounded the palm of his hand against the steering wheel. "What the hell is wrong with me?" he growled, pulling away from Liberty's apartment complex.

He had almost kissed her. What had he been thinking? It was as if his mind had blocked out what she had done to him. The last couple of hours with her, all he saw was the woman he had once loved. The woman he had planned to marry. The woman he wanted to protect. But how could he have forgotten why she was off limits, even for a moment?

"It was those damn eyes…and those frickin' pouty lips…and that curvy-ass body. Shit. I am so screwed," he grumbled, unable to push aside the vision of her. The wall he had built where she was concerned started crumbling even more seeing the way she took care of Yvonne and Arthur. She had always been the type of person to step in whenever she saw a need, but she seemed to especially have a soft spot for this elderly couple. Nate hadn't realized it before, but she and his sister-in-law had some of the same characteristics.

He had to laugh, thinking about the hard time he had given Nick when he fell for his wife. He already knew that if his brother knew how messed up he was over Liberty, he would never let him hear the end of it.

Liberty. Damn. I'm even calling her by her new name.

Nate switched the radio to a hip-hop station, turning the volume up as loud as he could stand it. Maybe listening to Jay Z rap about having ninety-nine problems could drown out the thoughts of the *one* woman who could bring Nate to his knees. After all this time of hating her from afar, it had taken spending most of the day with her to wipe away some of the animosity. Was he crazy? Or was he just a glutton for punishment? He wasn't sure, but he needed to do something to take his mind off the woman.

A short while later, Nate pulled up to the security gate of the housing community where his cousin, Jerry, lived. He punched in the code, and when the visitor's gate opened, he drove through and followed the main road around to Jerry's street.

Summer was definitely different than the fall and winter months in Cincinnati. Seemed everyone was outside taking advantage of the warm weather. Even as the sun began to set, some residents, young and old, were hanging out by the large pool area in the middle of the complex. Children playing and screaming on the nearby jungle gym also snagged his attention.

Nate parked in front of Jerry's two-car garage and climbed out of his vehicle. Jerry had called earlier, reminding Nate that they'd planned to shoot pool. Initially, Nate had thought about canceling, but when he realized he was falling for Liberty again, he thought better of it. Otherwise, who knew when he would have left her place. He had already messed up when he held her hand while driving her home. He still didn't know what possessed him to touch her. Maybe it was the pensive look on her face or the tension bouncing off of her as they drove. Whatever it was made him forget to keep his distance.

Nate strolled up the short walkway that led to Jerry's door and knocked. Instead of Jerry's door opening, the one behind Nate opened. He turned just as a nice-looking woman in her mid-thirties along with a cute little girl walked out.

The woman gave a shy smile and said hello. While she locked the townhouse door, the little girl, who Nate assumed was her daughter, walked up to him. The long ponytails on each side of her head bounced with every step.

"Are you Jerry's friend?" she asked, her gorgeous brown eyes bright and innocent.

"Stormy, what did I tell you?" the mother scolded.

Stormy. Interesting.

Nate was sure there was a story behind the name. He didn't even know the little girl, but already he could tell she had a vibrant personality, opposite of any type of storm.

Stormy pouted, lowering her head. "You said I can't talk to strangers, but he's not one. He's Jerry's friend."

"Actually, I'm Jerry's cousin, Nate." He held out his hand and shook hers. When she smiled up at him, Nate knew she was going to be a heartbreaker when she got older.

Jerry's door swung open. "What's up, man? I see you met my future wife and my ladybug."

Nate's brow quirked up, surprised at his cousin's words. The same cousin who vowed he'd never give up his player's card for any woman. A quick glance at Stormy's mother and Nate caught her rolling her eyes. If her annoyed expression was any indication, his cousin had his work cut out for him if he planned to win this woman's heart. So far, she clearly hadn't fallen for his infamous charm. Unlike the mother, Stormy squealed in delight at seeing Jerry.

"Hi, Jerry!" Excitement bounced off of her like fireworks lighting up the sky. She leaped into his arms.

"Ladybug, did you meet my cousin?"

She nodded vigorously. "His name is…um," she frowned before grinning, "Nate!" Nate and Jerry laughed at her enthusiasm.

"Wait, I thought your name was Stormy," Nate said, aware that the mother hadn't acknowledge Jerry, but stood in the walk-way fiddling with her keys.

"That is my name. Jerry said I'm his ladybug." She placed her short arms around Jerry's neck and gave him a noisy kiss on the cheek. Anyone looking in from the outside would've thought the pair were father and daughter considering she favored him a little. Clearly, they were fond of each other which was no surprise since all the Jenkins men loved children. "Do you know why he calls me ladybug?" Stormy asked Nate.

"No. Why does he call you that?"

"Because I like ladybugs."

Nate also noticed that Jerry's gaze kept drifting to the mother. She was definitely his type, pretty, stylishly dressed with full breasts and big hips. He loved thick women, claiming there wasn't a thing he could do with a sack of bones.

"Okay, Stormy, we have to get going. Let's leave Jerry to his company."

Jerry didn't set Stormy down. He moved past Nate and carried her to the car.

"You know if you want to come over for dinner, I'll get rid of him," Jerry said to the mother, nodding his head toward Nate. Nate almost burst out laughing. That was so like his cousin. He wouldn't care if all the guys were hanging out at his house. Let a woman want to come over, he'd have them out of there in a heartbeat.

Jerry opened the back passenger door and placed Stormy in the car seat. When he closed the door, he turned to the woman who was standing near the trunk of the car.

"Just say the word. I'll get us a babysitter and then you can have your way with me."

She rolled her eyes again and shook her head. "Whatever, Jerry. I'm sure whatever woman you're hooking up with tonight is more interested in you than I am."

Jerry slammed his hand over his heart. "Dang, Rayne, you wound me."

Rain? As in rain…storm? What the heck is up with the weather names.

Instead of going into the house and giving them some privacy, Nate stayed put. They were more entertaining than some of the latest TV sitcoms.

"Why do you insist on always stomping on my feelings?" Jerry asked her, doing a pitiful job of looking wounded. When he tugged on the front of her shirt and she let him pull her a little closer, it almost seemed he had her attention. Until he said, "You know I love you."

"Bye, Jerry," she said, irritation dangling from the word. She nodded at Nate before climbing into her old Chevy. After several attempts, the car finally started.

"What the hell was that all about?" Nate asked when he followed Jerry into the townhouse.

Instead of going up the stairs, they stepped into the first-floor bedroom where a pool table took up the middle of the floor. Jerry referred to the space as his game room. He had a flat screen TV on a far wall hooked up to a gaming station, as well as a dart board on another wall. The small refrigerator and cabinet above it held plenty of drinks and snacks.

Nick racked the pool balls. "I've never heard you joke about marrying anyone."

His cousin took a long time to respond as he chalked one of the pool cues. "I don't know what's wrong with me. She makes me say shit like that. It just slipped out."

"By her reaction, I assume you talk nonsense all the time."

"Can't help it. There's just something about the woman. I can't put my finger on it, but she makes me want to try a monogamous relationship."

"Get the hell out of here. For real?"

"Do I look like I'm kidding? Problem is, Rayne always turns me down. Can you believe that shit?"

Nate stared at his cousin and then burst out laughing, unable to help himself. Unless he was arguing or fighting with someone, Jerry was rarely serious. But he was standing on the other side of the pool table, shock written all over his face. It was as if the thought of anyone turning down his advances were unheard of.

It took Nate a good five minutes to gather his composure. It didn't help that Jerry's expression was of that of someone who had just lost their best friend.

"I take it she's had a front row seat to your revolving door of women."

"That can't be it. It's been months since I've brought anyone back here. Not since Rayne and ladybug moved in almost four months ago. So I'm not sure why she won't give me any play."

"You're serious?"

"As a heart attack. She's the one for me, man. I just have to figure out how to get her attention."

Nate didn't know what to say. Jerry had never been serious about any one woman before, but Nate had his own woman problems. He wasn't in a position to give anyone advice.

"Looked like you and Stormy were pretty tight. How old is she?"

His cousin's whole face lit up in a smile. "Yeah that's my heart. She'll be five in a few months, and she's as smart as a whip. She told me she wants to be an electrician when she grows up."

Nate laughed. His cousin might've been a screw up in some cases, but he was one of the best electricians in the city. And considering how he was going on about the mother and daughter, Jerry was definitely taken with the pair.

"All right, enough about me. What's up with your girl?"

"She's not my girl."

A slow grin spread across his cousin's face. "If she's not, how did you know who I was talking about?"

Nate released an irritated sigh. "Do you want to break or what?" he asked, ignoring the comment as he removed the rack from around the pool balls on the table.

Jerry went to the other end of the table and lined up the cue ball. Nate wasn't ready to talk about Liberty. Heck, what could he say? *I'm falling for a woman who ripped my heart out once and might do it again.*

"So you guys were pretty tight until she up and married some rich punk, huh?" Jerry asked after breaking the balls, sending them scattering all over the table. When two striped ones dropped into the pockets he said, "At least I can see why you fell for her. The woman is *hot*."

Nate frowned, not sure how he felt about his cousin referring to Liberty as *hot*. She was definitely a looker, but it was too weird knowing others noticed. "I guess I don't have to ask where you got your information." Nick was the only one, besides their father, who knew why he and Liberty parted ways.

"Don't be mad at Nick. After you stared the woman down and then carried her out of the bar last night, we all figured there was some serious history between you two. So now that she's back, what are you going to do?"

"I have no idea," Nate said without hesitation, watching as his cousin sank another ball before missing his next shot.

"It's obvious you still care about her. I say go for it."

"Of course you would now that you've found the love of your life," Nate cracked. "But some decisions aren't that easy to make."

"Well, like a wise person once told me, *until you make a decision, nothing is going to happen.*"

"And who told you that?" Nate asked, lining up his next shot.

"It was just something from a book."

Nate glanced up in surprise. "Since when did you start reading?"

Jerry's brows drew together. "Hell, I read!" he snapped with indignation, but dropped the attitude when Nate gave him a *yeah, right* look. "Okay maybe Rayne told me, but still. It's good advice."

Nate fell out laughing. Stopping by Jerry's place was turning out to be a good decision. Nate had a feeling he'd be laughing for the rest of the evening. Just what his troubled mind needed.

Chapter Twelve

Liberty sat at the round table in Nate's office, listening as he, Nick, and their cousin Toni argued about her not wearing one of the J & S company shirts. Instead, she wore a T-shirt that boasted: *The only thing more badass than a plumber is a woman plumber.*

Toni claimed she only wore the attire to work when scheduled to help in the office, but Nate, and especially Nick, insisted it wasn't a professional look.

"Fine! I'll save these shirts for when I'm not working. Are you happy now?" Toni snapped, folding her arms across her chest. "Jeez, the way you two are acting, you would think I had a marijuana plant or a joint on the shirt. What do you think, Liberty? Are you offended by what it says?"

Liberty's brows shot up as three sets of eyes zeroed in on her. "Um…um nooo, I'm not offended by it." She held up her hand to stop Toni from getting too excited. "*But*, I have to agree with the guys. It's not very professional for the office."

"Okay, then it's settled. Only company shirts going forward," Nick said, pinning Toni with a firm glare.

Sorry, Liberty mouthed to Toni, who gave her a small smile and waved off the apology.

This was Liberty's first time meeting the petite plumber and she liked her immediately. The four of them had gathered to work on a part of the proposal that needed Nick and Toni's input. For the past hour, they discussed concerns and reevaluated the proposed budget for the Unity Tower project. Though the work was serious, it had been fun watching Toni's interaction with the brothers. They treated her more like a little sister than their cousin, all the while accepting her input and respecting her suggestions.

Also during the last couple of weeks, Liberty had an opportunity to watch how the twins interacted. Nate and Nick were fraternal twins, but except for their skin tone, they looked identical. Nate was a rich dark chocolate, while Nick had more of a milk chocolate skin tone. Some of their mannerisms were similar, but Nate was a little more polished, gentler and calmer, while Nick seemed quick to snap and had a rougher edge to him. With the tattoos covering his arms, he definitely had a bad-boy vibe going on. If Liberty had met them both at the same time, she had no doubt Nate still would've been the one to grab her attention first. There was something so addictive about the man that years apart hadn't suppressed.

Liberty tuned back into the conversation with the cousins. Toni explained why she thought they needed to add more of a cushion to the proposed completion schedule for the project. Over the past hour, she had definitely earned Liberty's respect with her knowledge of the construction industry and her ability to fit in easily within a male dominated environment.

"All right, I think that's all we needed from you guys," Nate said to Nick and Toni. "Me and Liberty will tweak the proposed time-line to accommodate for J&S schedule. Oh, and I noted that LCA will pull all required permits."

Liberty nodded and double-checked that she had indeed added that information. "Got it."

For the past couple of weeks, she and Nate had spent a few hours each day pecking away at the proposal. They had at least three more working meetings before they would be ready to submit. Considering how they started off, Liberty hadn't expected them to work so well together. After talking for hours, following her drunken stupor, it was as if they hadn't lost thirteen years.

She looked up to find Nate staring at her, something he'd been doing a lot of lately. She held his gaze for a moment, her body thrumming with awareness. With just a look, he had the ability to make her feel things she hadn't felt in years. Even when they dated in college, he'd been so in tune with her that she could easily forget anyone else was around. Her desire to get reacquainted with him built with each passing day they spent together.

"Damn, why don't you two just get a room already," Nick said and stood.

"I agree. I think that's our cue to cut out and give them some privacy," Toni added, standing as well. "Those heated looks you guys have been sharing is enough to burn down the whole building."

Warmth surged to Liberty's cheeks and she glanced down at her laptop, shocked that anyone had noticed. Just once she would love to spend time at J & S without embarrassing herself.

"Don't let them get to you, Liberty. My family is known for saying whatever is on their mind. Do like I do. Ignore them."

"Yeah, whatever," Toni said. Liberty looked up as Toni and Nick headed to the door. "Oh, and nice meeting you Liberty, even if you don't like my shirt." She smiled with those last words, letting Liberty know she was kidding.

"Well, I'm heading out. See you guys later. If you need me, hit me up on my cell phone."

When Nick walked out, Liam showed up in the doorway. Tall with a runner's build and dark soulful eyes, he was handsome like the other Jenkins men Liberty had met. He wasn't as well built or as sexy as Nate, but she could be biased. She had tried keeping those old, romantic feelings for him at bay, but each day they spent together, they grew closer.

"Sorry to interrupt guys, but Nate, did you have a chance to rework the numbers for the Grisham assignment?"

"Yep, all done. I had planned to email you the information this morning, but it totally slipped my mind."

"I guess with the beautiful distraction sitting next to you, I can see why."

"I know, right? It's a wonder I've been able to accomplish anything lately." Nate smiled without looking up from his laptop and Liberty's whole body flushed. Hanging out with them was good for her ego. She couldn't remember the last time someone referred to her as beautiful.

"Okay, I just emailed you the changes."

"Cool. Thanks. I'm out of here. Take care Liberty."

"Thanks, you too," she said as he closed the door.

"How about we knock off and grab an early dinner?" Nate asked.

He stood and stretched his arms high above his head, his shirt pulling tight against his muscular form. Liberty tried not to stare, but the man's body was a work of art even sheathed in clothes. Dressed down in a beige polo shirt that fit snug over his muscular chest, his biceps bulged against the sleeves. She didn't know when he had time to work out, but his thick arms and flat abs were sure signs of someone who had a strict fitness regimen. She yearned to run her hands up and down his beautiful dark skin and feel his well-honed muscles ripple beneath her touch.

"So you interested?" Nate asked with a raised eyebrow.

Liberty's eyes widened. Wait. What? Was he propositioning her? "Um…interested?" she stammered.

"Dinner. You and me."

"Oh. Yeah, right, dinner," she said, embarrassed at the route her thoughts had taken her. Of course, he wasn't talking about anything other than food. What the heck was wrong with her? The last few times they'd met, her mind conjured up one fantasy after another with him being the main star.

They might have been getting along fine, but no way was he interested in anything but finishing the proposal. She didn't even know if he had finally forgiven her for walking out on him in college. If the way he'd been treating her lately was any indication, she would guess yes. But Liberty didn't want to assume. She didn't want to come right out and ask him since she wasn't prepared for a negative response.

"Sure, dinner sounds fine." She glanced at her watch surprised that it was already five o'clock. She didn't really have extra money to eat out, but she couldn't pass up a chance to spend more time with Nate. That would win out every time over going home on a Friday night to an empty apartment.

Thirty minutes later, she pulled into the parking lot of Kendricks' Seafood & Steak House. Liberty had insisted on driving her own vehicle to the downtown restaurant instead of riding with Nate. She used the excuse that the restaurant was closer to her apartment, and it didn't make sense for him to have to drive her back to her car. But that wasn't the only reason she preferred to drive. Lately, she thought about Nate morning, noon, and night. Riding in the car with him would've felt too personal. Like they were more than business associates. Already spending so much time with him was messing with her mind and her libido. Bringing back memories of what they once had, and dreams of what could've been. If it were possible to do her life over again, Nate would definitely be at the center of it.

"But you don't get a redo," Liberty murmured and pulled into the first parking space she found.

By the time Liberty parked, Nate was at her driver's side door. She undid the locks and he opened the door, extending his hand to help her out of the vehicle. How was she going to keep from falling for him again when he kept doing things like this? Isaac had started off being gentlemanly, but he stopped trying in their marriage when he figured out she was still in love with Nate.

"I'm starving," Nate said as they walked toward the restaurant. "Did I mention that Martina's husband owns the place?"

"Wow, no you didn't." Nate explained how Paul Kendricks had been a state senator who loved to cook and wanted to one day own his own restaurant. After he and Martina married, he hadn't run for a new term and chose to oversee his restaurant and start planning for expansion.

Liberty had officially met Martina a few days ago. She'd been nice enough, but the little amount of time they'd spent together she feared Martina would comment on that day in Nate's office when Liberty fell apart. She hadn't, but she kept looking at Liberty with a Cheshire cat grin as if she had a big secret.

Nate pulled open the glass door, allowing Liberty to enter first. The sensational smell of food, as well as friendly chatter greeted them when they walked in. Standing just inside the entrance, Liberty took in the chic interior with a wood planked ceiling similar to the one in Nate's family room. The fancy light fixtures emitting a soft glow over the room made the black and white photos pop against the sparkling walls. Soft jazz playing through the speakers added to the ambiance of the large space.

Most of the tables and booths were already occupied despite it being fairly early for a dinner crowd. Even the semicircular bar was congested with people occupying the bar stools and those standing close by. Thinking there was a waiting list, Liberty spotted a seat in the small entrance area where others were sitting.

"Where you going?" Nate whispered, stopping her with a hand on her arm.

"I figured since we'll have to wait, I'd grab that seat over there." She pointed to the leather bench where two women were sitting.

"There's a family dining room in back reserved for the Jenkins and the Kendricks whenever needed. It's empty and waiting for us, unless you'd prefer to eat in the main dining room."

Eying the hostess holding two menus waiting for them, Liberty flashed a small smile. *Alrighty then.*

"Nope. That works for me."

Liberty learned more and more about the Jenkins family every day. The grandparents had built the construction company from nothing to give their family members a good start in life. Nate made it clear that none of them were forced to work for the family business, but most of the grandkids had their first jobs with the company. When the grandfather, Steven Jenkins, was ready to retire, Nate's cousin, Peyton, had taken over. Thanks to her, the company had become a multi-million-dollar operation. Liberty had already been impressed with what she'd learned about the company, but knowing that a woman, who was also an electrician, had grown the business, impressed her even more.

Nate's large hand settled at the small of Liberty's back, and that electric tingling sensation invaded her body again as they followed the hostess through the main dining room. His powerful presence, his touch, and everything else about the man continued to do wicked things to her body. How was she going to get through dinner without wanting to hug him, kiss him, and go even further with him?

Just settle down, she thought and noticed the attention they garnered, especially from women checking out Nate. He was hard to miss. At over six feet tall with wide shoulders, and handsome enough to grace the cover of a magazine, if she were them, she would take a second and third look too.

"Here we are." The hostess stepped aside to let them enter a beautifully decorated room. It was large enough to hold several round tables, but small enough to give a cozy feel. The wall of windows on the opposite side of the room gave a view of a courtyard with a waterfall and stone benches around it.

"Perfect. Thanks, Donna," Nate said and pulled a chair out for Liberty. The hostess left them with a couple of menus before closing the door behind her.

Liberty settled in and perused the menu, taking in the prices of the entrees. They were a little steep for her budget, so she checked out the salad selection.

"Do you eat seafood?" Nate asked, his menu lying flat on the table.

She shook her head. "Maybe I'll just get a salad."

"I'm sure you eat enough salads. Kendricks' has several vegetarian appetizers and entrees."

"I didn't really come prepared to eat out today," Liberty said honestly, hoping he'd understand that the restaurant was out of her price range.

Nate studied her before speaking. "Liberty, I wouldn't have invited you to dinner if I wasn't planning to pay for it. I'm not that guy."

She wasn't sure if he was speaking of a particular guy, like Isaac. Or if he was speaking in general. Either way, she knew he was different than any man she'd ever met. Even with their years apart, he was still the sweet, generous gentleman she remembered.

"Order whatever you want, but I'd recommend the veggie enchiladas or the eggplant lasagna. They're amazing." He grinned and Liberty returned his smile. The past couple of weeks hanging around Nate had been better than she expected. Her only concern was that she could get used to his attentiveness. They worked well together and he went beyond the call of duty catering to her. For their morning meetings, he made sure there was a cup of coffee ready for her along with a variety of juices. If they met around lunchtime, he always ordered her a salad or some other vegetarian dish and had it at the office by the time she arrived. Those small gestures went a long way with her.

"Okay. I'll try the eggplant lasagna."

"Hey, nephew."

They glanced toward the door and Nate smiled at the friendly, older woman coming toward them with a small note pad. Liberty wasn't sure who she was, but she favored the actress Holly Robinson Peete. She glided into the room as if on a cloud and her vibrant smile was contagious.

"Hey, Aunt Cat. What are you doing here?" Nate stood and kissed her cheek.

"A couple of servers called in, and since I wasn't doing anything," she shrugged, "I figured I'd help out. Who's your friend?"

"This is Liberty Stewart. Liberty, this is my aunt Carolyn Richwood, Martina's mother."

Nate explained that she used to be a bartender at the restaurant, but quit after getting married almost a year ago.

"Pleasure to meet you, Liberty."

"Same here."

"So, what can I get you two?"

Carolyn took their order and they all talked for a few minutes. Liberty loved what appeared to be a fun relationship between Nate and his aunt. She had a great sense of humor and seemed so down to earth. Liberty had been close to some of her extended family before going off to college, but had distanced herself from them when they didn't come through for her parents. When she was a kid, she dreamed of having a large family of her own, but considering the way her life turned out, that desire would be—a dream.

Once Carolyn left to place their order, Liberty said, "She seems really nice."

"She's the best. Like you, she's had some tough breaks but it takes a lot to keep Aunt Cat down. Some of the men she dated in the past were a little sketchy." Nate chuckled. "But Lincoln is cool. He's the first guy she hooked up with, as far as I know, who is actually her age. Normally the men were like ten years younger than her. Aunt Cat and Lincoln eloped after Christmas last year and she's been happier than I've ever seen her."

A server returned with their drinks. While she chatted with Nate, Liberty thought about what he'd said about his aunt and her bad breaks. If Carolyn could find love again, maybe there was a chance for her, Liberty thought. After her divorce, she hadn't wanted anything to do with men and hadn't entertained the idea of ever being in a serious relationship again. Until now. Until Nate. He had her imagining what it would be like to be in a loving relationship.

Nate's laughter cut into Liberty's thoughts. "Thanks again for the drinks, and tell your brother we need to get back on the golf course."

"I'll be sure to tell him," the server said on her way out the door.

"Do you think you'll ever get married?" The words were out of Liberty's mouth before she could stop them, but she let them hang out there because she really wanted to know.

Nate took a long swig of his beer, his gaze steady on her as he set the glass down. "I hope so. I thought I'd be married by now with a few children, but so far it hasn't happened. What about you? Do you think you'd ever get married again?"

Liberty ran her fingers along her water glass, wiping away some of the condensation. "Nate, if you would've asked me a year ago, heck, even six months ago, I would've said *hell* no."

He chuckled and drank more of his beer. "But now?"

"Now, I don't know. But if I ever do, I'll be marrying for love." She looked him in the eye. "I missed out once. I'll never make that mistake again."

Nate nodded, but didn't comment on her response. Instead he asked, "How do you like Cincinnati?"

"It's no Chicago." She laughed. "Yet, so far Cincinnati has been a good move for me. It was past time for a change."

"Well," he lifted his glass to her and she raised hers, "I'm glad you're here."

Liberty smiled believing that he really meant it. "Me too." They tapped glasses just as Carolyn and another server brought in their food.

Once their food arrived, they laughed and talked like old friends. After breaking up with Isaac, Liberty had lost the few acquaintances she'd made while being married. Watching her so-called friends turn on her and believe the nonsense that Isaac was feeding to the media made her sick. Until now, she didn't realize how much she missed hanging out and sharing a meal with someone, especially a man.

"I've been wanting to ask you something," Nate said, hesitation in his tone.

"What?"

"Did you finish law school? Did you pass the bar?"

Liberty moved lasagna around on her plate. The questions were simple, but there was still so much Nate didn't know about her. Tonight wasn't the time for another deep conversation.

"Yes, I have my law degree, but no, I haven't taken the bar."

As if sensing some hesitation, he asked, "Why do I feel as if there's a story there and it involves Isaac?"

Liberty nodded. "There is, but…maybe we can talk about it another time."

"I'm going to hold you to that."

Liberty laughed. "I'm sure you are."

"Tell me, what do you usually do after work?" Nate asked between bites.

"Not much. My boss has given me more projects. Some nights I work until I can't keep my eyes open. Other nights I sit in front of the television and watch reality shows while vegging out on carrot and celery sticks."

"I think you need to get out more."

"Ya think?" They laughed and Liberty's heart swelled. She and Nate had been friends before they became lovers in college. Spending time with him she realized how much she missed having him as a friend.

A cell phone vibrated and she reached for her handbag in the chair next to her.

"It's mine," Nate said digging his phone from his pants pocket. He glanced at the screen. "Sorry. I need to take this. I'll be right back."

"Okay." Liberty watched him head to the door, taking in how good his ass looked encased in a pair of dress pants. Firm. Round. He had the type of butt that was perfect for making love. Not flat but one that she could hold onto each time he entered...

"Oh my, God." Her heart slammed against her chest. "What is wrong with me?"

Liberty hadn't had sex in almost six years. Not since she and Isaac had stop sleeping together long before they divorced. This was the first time she'd even entertained the thought of making love with anyone since then and with Nate no less.

Sighing loudly, she reached for her glass of water. Coming to dinner with him was a bad idea. A very bad idea. She had already started dreaming about him again, like she used to do when they first parted ways. Why torture herself by spending more time with him? He had already made it clear that he wasn't interested in anything more than a working relationship.

But a girl can dream though.

Chapter Thirteen

"Hey, Uncle Ben. Tell me you heard something about the land," Nate said regarding land that he and his uncle had bid on. They had recently joined forces and started a property development company. This property would be their first purchase under the new venture. When his uncle started talking, Nate could barely hear him. "Hold on a sec."

Music and conversations from the main dining room drifted in Nate's direction, and he glanced around for a quieter spot. He headed around the corner and stopped near the restrooms.

"Okay, what did you say?"

"They didn't accept our offer, nor did they counter, but it might be a blessing in disguise. I heard from a reliable source that the property on Fairway Lane is going on the market in a couple of weeks."

"Wait. The one that overlooks California Golf Course?"

"That would be the one. It'll only be five acres, but I'm thinking if we tweak our initial plans, it could work. I'll see if I can get an appointment with the owner for next week sometime."

"Sounds good. Just text me the..." Nate's voice trailed off when the women's bathroom door swung open. Angel stopped short, her surprised expression probably mirrored his. What were the chances of him running into her? A slow smile tilted her lips upward. "Sorry, Uncle Ben, I have to go, but text me the day and time and I'll make myself available," he said before ending the call.

"Hey, Nate. I was going to call you. Are we still on for tomorrow night?" Angel asked, catching him off guard when she quickly touched her lips to his.

"What the hell, Angel!" Nate snapped, stepping away as he wiped his mouth with the back of his hand. The last thing he needed was to walk into the room to Liberty with another woman's lipstick on his mouth.

"What?" The innocent expression on her face had him wondering if something was mentally wrong with the woman. She closed the gap between them. "I can't kiss my man when I see him?"

"I'm *not* your man. Never have been. *Never* will be. What's your problem? I've made it clear—I'm not interested." At the moment, there was only one woman he was interested in, and she was sitting in a room, a few feet away, waiting on him.

"So, you're telling me that you're passing on all of this?" Her hands flowed down her body bringing attention to the way the short yellow sundress hugged her curvaceous body.

Nate could admit that she was a stunning woman, but he had never been the type of man to go for looks alone. He took the whole package into consideration.

He and Angel had met two months ago through mutual friends. At first, Nate thought she was nice and he was interested in getting to know her. After a few dates, that changed. She was possessive and clingy. When she began talking about marriage, he knew he had to cut all ties.

"Angel, clearly there's a communication breakdown between us. We had a nice time, but there is no us." He swung his hand back and forth between them. "We talked about this. It's best if we go our separate ways, and I don't know how else to make that clear to you."

Angel shook her head, ready to protest when a male's voice called out her name. She glanced over her shoulder at a man about Nate's height, with a linebacker build approaching them. He wasn't too happy if the glare directed at Nate was any indication.

"I was wondering what happened to you." He wrapped his arm around Angel's waist, kissing her on the cheek. She visibly stiffened with an awkward smile plastered on her face.

Hmm…interesting. If she was at the restaurant with a date, why had she kissed him?

"I was on my way to the table," Angel said to her date, easing out of his hold and casting a freakishly sweet smile at Nate and then touched his arm. "I got sidetracked when I ran into Nate. I wanted to thank him for the flowers he'd sent."

All types of warning bells sounded inside of Nate's head. What flowers? The woman really was crazy. Unless…she was trying to make this guy jealous.

"I never sent you flowers, Angel." Whatever game she was playing, he wanted nothing to do with it.

When she narrowed her eyes at him, her jaw clenched, Nate knew he had made the right decision to cut her loose.

"Come on. Let's get out of here." The linebacker started leading her away, but not before he turned back and glared at Nate.

"Two women, Nate? Really?" Carolyn came up behind him. Nate thought he had heard the door to the second level open before Angel's little game started. When he didn't hear or see anyone, he hadn't thought anything else about the sound. The floor above was where Paul's office was located.

"How much did you hear?"

"Enough to wonder if you're juggling a couple of women."

Nate shook his head. "I'm a one-woman man. Angel is someone from my past who doesn't seem to understand that I'm not interested in her. And for the record, I never sent her flowers and we only went out a handful of times."

"I see. What about the one you're having dinner with?"

"She's someone…" He paused to decide how he wanted to describe Liberty. "She's someone I'm interested in getting to know better."

Carolyn nodded. "Well, I suggest you be careful with Ms. Yellow Dress because the daggers that girl was shooting with her eyes could amputate a body part."

"I'll keep that in mind."

Nate reentered the family dining room. "Sorry, I didn't mean for that to take so long."

Liberty looked up from her cell phone. "No problem. I was just catching up on emails. Give me one second to finish this response."

Nate reclaimed his seat, studying her as she tapped away on the device. Smooth skin the color of chestnuts shone under the lights and he longed to touch her. The white, sleeveless blouse showed off her long, graceful neck, perky breasts and toned arms. She definitely wasn't the young, skinny girl he dated back in college, but a beautiful woman who had experienced a rough life and survived.

After all these years, there was still just something about her that called to him. Nate was falling for her all over again. At first, he thought the strong attraction was him adhering to the damsel in distress scenario his brother often called him out on. But this was different. The intense pull that drew him to her like a magnet to steel couldn't be ignored.

"Why are you looking at me like that?" Liberty asked, interrupting his thoughts.

Nate met her gaze. "You're still one of the most beautiful women I've ever known."

Her brows shot up and she pointed to herself. "Me?" The surprise in her voice along with the nervous laugh made him think that she didn't know just how attractive she was.

"Yes, you. Why do you find that so hard to believe?"

"Because… I find it hard to believe that I can even compare to the women you know. You're a hot, good-looking man. Gorgeous women are probably coming out of the woodwork to get with you."

Just not the right ones, Nate thought and then smiled. "You think I'm hot, huh?"

She laughed and it was as if a dark cloud was pushed out of the way by the sun. Her whole face lit up and suddenly he didn't see the sadness that had been lingering in her eyes for the past couple of weeks.

For the next hour, they talked and laughed like old times. As they spent time together, memories of what they'd shared all those years ago filled his mind. Good memories. Memories of how he used to walk her to class and then sprint to his own class to keep from being late. Memories of his lips covering hers in heated kisses. Memories of how responsive she was to his touch. Even now he could almost feel her shivering against him, moaning with every trace of his fingers along her body.

"Nate?"

Nate blinked several times as Liberty waved her hand in front of his face.

"Where'd you go? Am I boring you?" she asked, a teasing smile on her lips that made him want to kiss her and see if they were as sweet as he remembered.

He chuckled. "On the contrary. I'm enjoying your company. As a matter of fact, I'd like to take you out again. What does your weekend look like?"

Liberty shrugged. "Besides doing a little work, I don't have anything planned."

"Would you like to go out with me?"

Her face broke out into a smile. "That would be nice."

Nate took care of the check while they discussed possible things they could do on their date. He had wanted to ask her out before now, but there was still a bit of uncertainty nagging at him. Questioning whether seeing her on a personal level was a good idea.

"Ready to go?" he asked.

"Yes."

They headed to the door and when Nate had his hand on the door knob, he stopped and turned to Liberty. Before he could talk himself out of his next move, he covered her mouth with his and the softness of her lips had his senses reeling. He hadn't planned to kiss her, and there hadn't been any real motivation behind his invitation to Kendricks except for dinner. Yet, the last couple of hours with her had his body burning with desire.

After a slight hesitation, Liberty opened for him, her tongue touching his tentatively before she returned his kiss with an eagerness that matched his. It was when she moaned against his mouth that Nate knew he was a goner.

He buried his fingers into her thick hair as he increased the pressure. This woman…even after all the years of separation, kissing her still felt like home. Her luscious body moved against him and no doubt she felt his erection pressing against her. He knew he should probably let her up for air, but she felt so perfect in his arms and he wanted more, so much more.

The initial shock of having Nate's mouth covering hers was quickly replaced with a raging desire Liberty hadn't felt in years. She never thought she would have the pleasure of tasting him again, feeling his body hugged up against hers.

His kiss was insistent, powerful and her heart thumped wildly with every lap of his tongue. A whimper slipped from her when Nate tightened his hold around her waist. Though she wasn't a dainty woman, she felt like one next to him. He was so big and tall, making her feel delicate, desired and safe with his tenderness. Kissing him seemed like the most natural thing in the world to do. Like old times.

"God, I've missed you," he mumbled against her mouth moments before he lifted his head, shocking her with his declaration. With both of them breathing hard, he touched his forehead to hers while they caught their breaths.

"I've missed you too," she said ignoring the questions rattling her brain. She missed him more than he would ever know.

"I'm not going to apologize for kissing you," he said, his voice rough with desire.

"Me either." Not only wasn't Liberty going to apologize, she wanted a repeat, and then another, and yet another.

"Come on. We'll talk about our date this weekend while I walk you to your car."

Chapter Fourteen

"When you mentioned golf, I thought you meant miniature golf," Liberty said to Nate. He grunted something indiscernible as he pulled a set of golf clubs from the trunk of his SUV. At first his plan was to take her to an actual golf course until he found out she didn't know how to golf. That was how they ended up at the driving range.

"Nate, I don't think you'll be able to teach me how to play golf," Liberty said as she jogged to keep up with him. "I'm terrible at most sports. There's no way I'll be able to hit that little ball."

"Don't worry. You'll be fine."

Nate carried the golf clubs in one hand and surprised Liberty when his other hand reached for hers. So far their date was going great. They'd had a wonderful breakfast at a place not too far away and the whole morning felt like old times. Liberty didn't want to read too much into Nate's actions, but she couldn't help it. A few weeks ago, all she had wanted was for him to forgive her. She never dreamed they would be sharing meals, holding hands, and kissing.

God, his kisses.

The kiss at Kendricks the day before had rocked her to the core, leaving her wanting more. But the kisses they'd shared today were off the charts. It had been so long since

119

she'd been kissed, and she had forgotten how enjoyable they could be. Lips so soft but firm and in charge, even now it was as if she could still feel his mouth against hers.

Nate squeezed her hand and she glanced at him. "Thanks for coming out here with me."

She returned his smile but stopped short of telling him that the way he had her feeling, she was ready to go anywhere with him.

They walked across the crowded parking lot and onto grass. Considering the driving range was packed, they didn't have to wait long for a teeing space. Nate set his clubs down and then went to purchase what seemed like a thousand golf balls for them to hit.

"You ready?" he asked.

Liberty glanced around at the other golfers, marveling at how far they hit the ball into the open field. There was no way she could do that.

"No, actually, I'm not. I don't want to embarrass myself."

"Baby, we all had to start somewhere. Just give it a try. Today I'm only going to teach you the basics about swinging a golf club." He grabbed one from his golf bag. "There are numbers on the heads of each golf club that represent the club's loft. The higher the number, the higher the loft."

Nate introduced her to the various clubs and their roles while he hit one ball after another. All of his shots were straight down the middle of the field, and Liberty had a better understanding of what he meant by the club's loft. Some shots seemed to go up higher toward the sky, while others sliced through the air.

"My main goal today is to work on your hand placement on the club, as well as teach you the proper way to swing."

When he stepped behind her to help get her grip right, Liberty soaked up the attention. The patience he showed had her falling for him all over again. This was what she missed. Not only a man's attention, but Nate's attention. Hanging out, laughing, and sharing some teachable moments even if it centered around golf.

Liberty looked at the club she was holding. "This all sounds too complicated, Nate. Maybe you can teach me a different sport."

He shook his head. "Not until you learn how to play *this* sport. Once you pass the bar and start practicing law, you're going to want to know how to golf."

Shock seized Liberty as she stood there surprised by this sweet, unpredictable man. "What makes you think I'm going to…"

The tenderness in Nate's expression squeezed her heart. Maybe there was a possibility she could get a second chance with him. A second chance at happiness. Why else would he care about her future, her career, or anything she did going forward?

"Nate, when you say stuff like that, like you care… I—I don't know what to say." She blinked back tears, horrified at the overwhelming emotion gripping her.

Nate's brows dipped in confusion. He removed the golf club from her hand and returned it to the bag before pulling her into his arms. "What'd I say? I just assumed that with your new life, you'd get back on track with fulfilling your dream of becoming a lawyer."

"Man, Nate." Her voice was filled with tears, but she refused to let them fall. No way was she crying in front of him again. "You have no idea how much it means to me that you even remembered that I wanted to be a lawyer. And now you're trying to prepare me for what might come with that career by teaching me…golf of all things." She couldn't help laughing. There were so many other things she needed to be doing and learning to prepare for her future career. Golf definitely wasn't at the top of the list, but if learning the sport meant spending more time with him then she was all for it.

"All right. Teach me everything you know."

*

It was becoming even more evident that Isaac had really done a number on her. How could any man keep his woman from being the best she could be, and not encourage her to go after her dreams?

A part of Nate wanted to know what happened in her marriage that kept her from taking the bar. Yet, there was a bigger part of him that didn't want Isaac's name mentioned in any of their conversations.

"Why is golf such a big deal anyway when it comes to doing business?" Liberty asked once she pulled herself together.

She was so damn sexy, and the denim shorts and the low-cut, body hugging tank top, took her allure rating to a whole different level. All morning he had found every excuse to touch her, hold her, and kiss on her. He didn't know how much longer he'd be able to constrain himself from doing more with her.

"Business deals and some of the best connections are made on the golf course," he finally responded.

"Why do deals have to be made on the course, especially when it's so darn hot out here?"

She wiped sweat from her forehead with her forearm causing her tiny shirt to lift up. Seeing the bare skin of her midsection only increased Nate's desire. It *was* hot out there, and looking at her was only making him hotter. From the moment she had opened her apartment door, he'd had a semi-erection. The woman still had an effect on him and right now he wanted to do way more than just kiss her.

"I would imagine those same deals can be made over dinner."

"Maybe, but when you're playing golf, you're on the course for at least four or five hours. You're outside with a small group of people in a relaxed atmosphere. That's a big difference from sitting in a crowded restaurant with people at the next table close enough to hear your conversation."

Liberty nodded. "Okay, good point."

"Are you ready to give this a try?" Nate didn't wait for an answer. He pulled out a three iron and handed it to her. Then he set another golf ball on the tee. Despite her hesitancy, he pulled her onto the grass tee-box and stood behind her.

After a couple of shots, Nate knew bringing her to the driving range wasn't a good idea. Not because she missed a few balls. No, that wasn't it at all. It was her sweet ass rubbed up against the front of his body that caused his distress.

He released her arms and stepped back. "Okay, try it by yourself."

"Nate," she whined, but adjusted her grip on the golf club like he had shown her and swung.

She missed the ball the first two times, but nicked it the third time. Her frustration showed with each attempt, but she didn't complain.

"Okay," Nate said, placing another ball on the tee. "Remember, keep your eyes on the ball and make sure your left arm is straight when you bring the club back."

Nate moved behind her again and her fragrance was even more pronounce with the sun beaming down on them. Again, his body responded. Unable to help himself, he placed a quick kiss on her cheek and tried to get his head back into the lesson.

"Get your feet shoulder width apart and then soften your knees," he said as Liberty adjusted her grip on the golf club. Nate wrapped his arms around her and placed his hands over hers. "Damn you smell good." He inhaled next to her ear before placing soft kisses along her neck.

"Nate, I can't concentrate when you do that." Liberty squirmed against him as he continued kissing and nipping the length of her neck. "Nate," she dragged out his name. "Behave."

"Alright, alright, alright. Bend a little at the hip." When she did as told Nate cursed under his breath. She had to feel the effect she was having on him. "You keep moving like that, I won't be responsible for my actions."

She moaned and tilted her head to the left when he nipped at her earlobe. "Maybe I don't want you to be responsible."

That was all Nate needed to hear. "We're out of here."

Chapter Fifteen

Nate could barely get them into his house before they started stripping out of their clothes. First, their shirts were tossed, and then they toed off their shoes, rushing as if there was a fire at their backs. But when Nate had his hand on his belt buckle, he slowed, taking in the gorgeous woman he had spent the day with. Liberty stood before him in a white lace bra contrasting against her dark skin. He was sure that she had no idea what a sexy sight she made in the intimate apparel, her short-shorts, and her long, shapely legs. His gaze went lower to her bare feet adorned with hot pink nail polish on her toes.

Every animal instinct came alive within Nate, and he growled under his breath. His erection pressed painfully against his zipper, and he knew without a doubt he had to have her.

Liberty squealed when he lifted her off her feet. "Wrap your legs around me," he said, his voice rough with desire. He headed for his bedroom. Tempted to take her right there on the stairs, he scrapped the idea. He couldn't go all caveman with their first time.

Nate carried her up to his room and set her down next to the bed. Within seconds they had stripped out of the rest of their clothes. His body was on fire as his gaze traveled over her, appreciating her womanly curves that were on full display. He planned to kiss, lick, or bite every inch of her luscious body.

"You're absolutely breathtaking."

"Thank you," she said quietly, seeming a little unsure of herself at first, but then her gaze did its own exploration.

Liberty boldly stepped to him. Her small hands inched up his body, starting at his flat abs. Nate tried to stand still while she studied him, slowly working her fingers up his torso, to his pecks where she pinched one of his nipples.

He sucked in a breath at the tantalizing sting and the surprise move. Gone was the shy girl who used to share his bed in college. In her place was a gorgeous woman he couldn't wait to get reacquainted with.

"Your body is truly a work of art. More amazing than I imagined," she said, her exploratory touch sending shock waves to every nerve in his body. When her hand went lower, gripping his package, Nate knew he wouldn't be able to take this first time as slow as he had planned.

He unintentionally held his breath as she massaged him. With each stroke of her hand, he grew longer, harder, until he couldn't take any more. He covered her hand with his, halting the tantalizing assault.

"Too much of that and this will be over before we begin."

She smiled wickedly and loosened her grip. Nate backed her to the bed, and they climbed on. He covered her with his body, careful not to put all his weight on her. But when he stared down at her, he was momentarily caught off guard. Her expression had turned serious.

"Baby, if you're not ready for this tell me now."

"I'm ready." Liberty cupped his face. "It's just that...I've missed you. I've missed you so much, and I need you." She meant that in more ways than one. Being with him all day, experiencing the thoughtfulness he had showered on her, she had fallen for him completely. Liberty didn't think he had been trying to seduce her with the impromptu kisses, and his loving touches, but that's exactly what he had done. She hadn't been this turned on since the last time they were together.

Without another word, Nate's mouth lowered to hers. The man could kiss. Everything within her came alive with each stroke of his tongue, and Liberty knew being with him again was going to be like nothing she had ever experienced.

Her thoughts muddled when he moved from her mouth and littered kisses against her cheek and worked his way lower. He seared a slow path down the column of her neck, turning her on even more if that was possible.

When his mouth made its way back up to her lips, heat spread from the top of her head to the soles of her feet. She shivered as his hand roamed intimately over her breasts. The lust-arousing way he caressed her flesh while his tongue tangled with hers had her squirming against him. Never in a million years did she imagine being with him again. The feel of his mouth and his hands on her body while sharing his bed was truly a fantasy come true.

When his mouth replaced his fingers on one of her breasts, sucking, licking, teasing her relentlessly, Liberty practically crawled out of her skin. Arching her back to get even closer to him, she couldn't take much more. She hadn't been with a man in years, and she already felt the beginning of an orgasm.

Panting, she grabbed hold of his shoulders, her heart beating triple time as his mouth continued its delicious torture.

His hand slid down her side, rolled over the curve of her hip and then gripped her butt. The throb between her thighs grew more intense. With every kiss, each touch, and each lap of his tongue, Nate awakened the sexuality that had laid dormant inside of her for years. Her body was so starved for a man's attention, tremors of arousal began. Her mind jumbled at the sensual havoc he was causing to every nerve in her body.

"Nate," she gasped, unable to form another word as she wiggled beneath him. Right now she wanted to feel him inside of her more than she wanted to breathe.

"I'm with you, baby."

She needed him to move faster. Her breaths came in short spurts. The prolonged anticipation of their bodies joining as one was almost too much for her to stand.

As if sensing her distress, a slight grin touched his lips.

"Are you sure you're ready for me?" Not waiting for a response, he lowered his head. His wicked tongue swiped over one of her sensitive nipples, sending an electric current straight to her core.

"Nate…" She slammed her eyes shut, and a moan of ecstasy slipped through her lips. Her nails dug into his upper arms as he suckled each breast, flooding her body with a warmth she hadn't felt in years. She bucked against him, biting her lower lip to keep from crying out.

But it was when his hand eased between her thighs, and one finger then another slipped into her throbbing sex that she knew she was a goner.

Her hips moved on their own accord, and she bucked against his hand. His masterful fingers slid in and out, stroking, teasing her into a state of delirium. It was as if her body didn't belong to her as the erotic sensations pushed her closer to her release.

With one last stroke, an orgasm ripped through her, sending her into a tailspin. As she rode the wave of passion, it was as if all the drama that was once her life dissipated into thin air. She wanted to carry this feeling of content with her for the rest of her days.

Still breathing hard, her gaze met Nate's and her heart burst with love for the man she thought she would never be with again.

*

Nate kissed her tenderly but had no intention of letting her come down from her high. At least not until he was inside of her. Reaching into the top drawer of his nightstand, he grabbed a condom and quickly sheathed himself. Watching her explode like that had damn near done him in.

With a slight nudge of his legs, he spread her thighs wider and inched into her slick entrance. She was so tight. Her interior walls wrapped around him and Nate reveled in her sweetness.

He moved slowly, allowing her to adjust to his size. Everything within him wanted to go hard, but he didn't want to hurt her. He also wanted their time together to last forever. They found a rhythm that bound their bodies as one, and a wave of passion flowed between them. Being with Liberty like this exceeded his expectations, and all he could think was – *I'm never letting her go again.*

His body craved more of her, and he increased the pace, loving how she matched him stroke for stroke. Their moans filled the quietness of the room and Nate could feel the eagerness of her body course through his. But it was when she wrapped her long, smooth legs around his waist, making him go even deeper, that he knew he wouldn't be able to hang on much longer.

This woman. This beautiful, sexy woman was going to be the death of him with her erotic sounds and the way she moved beneath him. The faster he moved, the more she pulled him in, and the more out of control he felt.

He wasn't the only one on the brink. Liberty's grip on his arms tightened, and those erotic cries grew louder. Her head thrashed back and forth on the pillow, and her thighs trembled as she pulsed around his shaft.

Nate gritted his teeth not wanting this to end yet, but the pressure building inside of him was on the verge of exploding. And that's when she cried out. Shattering beneath him, her body shuddered, and he gave one last powerful thrust and was right behind her. A tide of fiery passion swirled within him, and he gave in to the force that took him over the edge.

Panting, Nate rested his forehead on the pillow next to her head, trying to catch his breath. He couldn't move but tried not to put all of his weight on her while he got his breathing under control.

Damn, that was intense.

Minutes ticked by, and Nate was about to ask if she was alright, but then she placed a lingering kiss against his jaw and sighed. No words were needed. At that moment it was as if all was right in his world.

Chapter Sixteen

After another round of lovemaking, Liberty lay cradled in Nate's arm, her head on his chest. Though a little sore, she couldn't ever remember feeling so sexually satisfied. Ever.

"How do you feel?" Nate asked, as if reading her mind, his hand caressing her hip.

"Amazing." His talented mouth and skilled hands had pleased her beyond anything she had ever experienced. Liberty didn't want to think about how Nate gained his proficiency in pleasing a woman, but he had learned well. The man had worshiped her body into complete submission.

"We got a little rough there. Are you sore?"

"A little." The slight ache between her legs was nothing when she considered the pleasure that came with the discomfort.

"Are you still a fan of bubble baths?"

Liberty smiled, touched that he remembered. Though her current bathroom was super small, she still preferred baths over showers. They just weren't as enjoyable. The tub wasn't very deep and there wasn't much space for candles.

"Some things haven't changed. I love them."

"I'll get the water started." Nate untangled himself and Liberty immediately missed his warmth. She watched him cross the room appreciating the view of his firm backside.

131

Her body stirred and the desire to go another round grew, but maybe he was right in them taking a short break.

Liberty turned onto her side toward the pair of windows. The past year had been one of the loneliest years of her life, but now, being there with Nate felt like a dream come true. The guilt she usually felt when she remembered how she had left him wasn't as strong. He hadn't actually come out and said he forgave her, but she knew him well enough to know that they wouldn't have had sex if he hadn't.

"Ready?" Nate asked from across the room.

Liberty turned to find him standing in the bathroom doorway still with no clothes on. Goodness, the man's body was a work of perfection. Yeah, she was ready alright, but for something even steamier than a bubble bath.

Instead of telling him that, she climbed out of bed and padded toward him, not missing the hunger in his eyes as he looked her up and down. He reached for her before she could pass by him.

"I had fun with you," he mumbled against her neck, sending desire racing through her body all over again. "How do you feel about me joining you for your bubble bath?"

She smiled, though taken aback by the question. "I would love that."

He led her into the bathroom and Liberty stopped short. She hadn't seen his bathroom, but it was bigger than her bedroom and more luxurious. The tray ceiling with a bamboo ceiling fan and similar material throughout, along with the dual vanities were gorgeous touches. As was the raised shower that required you to go up two steps to reach the all-glass enclosure. But it was the standalone soaking tub that was definitely the focal point.

The room was semi-dark. A single light over a leather bench in the corner of the bathroom and candles flickering on the vanities and on the wall shelves near the tub created a romantic feel. Soft jazz filled the space.

"Nate, this is...this is breathtaking. This room is by far my favorite spot in the house."

"I'm glad you like it." She followed him to the tub.

"Thank you for preparing the bath."

"My pleasure."

Once Nate was settled into the water, holding her hand, he guided her in. A woman could easily get used to the attention he'd been giving her. Sitting between his legs, she rested her back against him and sighed with contentment. The water a perfect temperature with bubbles everywhere soothed her to the bone.

"Any regrets about what we did this afternoon?" Nate asked, his voice quiet near her ear as his hand cupped one of her breasts, gently tweaking her nipple.

Liberty moan with pleasure. "No regrets." If anything, she wanted to do it over and over again, and never leave. But that might be asking too much. "What about you? Any regrets?" she asked, holding her breath.

"Not a one."

A classic instrumental by Grover Washington Jr. played through the speaker in the background. Sometimes Nate came off as an old soul, even his choice of music made her forget they were close in age. While they dated, he listened to jazz more than any other genre, not caring what some of his buddies thought.

Nate grabbed one of the wash cloths that was laying across the edge of the tub and dipped it into the water before running it across Liberty's chest. She closed her eyes and enjoyed the moment of him pampering her.

Neither of them spoke for the longest until Nate said, "I have a request."

She opened her eyes. "What's that?"

"No more secrets. I've learned more about you in the last few weeks that I should've known shortly after we started dating."

Yeah, she could say the same thing about him. Each time they got together, she discovered something new. Something that should've come out in college.

"I'd like to keep seeing you," he said, a slight hesitation in his tone. "I want us to get to know each other again. How do you feel about that?"

Liberty never imagined that they'd get a second chance, but was she ready? She was still trying to put her life back together. Could she be all that Nate needed? He had already proven that he was everything she wanted. If she waited until her life was perfect before getting into another relationship, she might miss out on the only man she'd ever loved.

"I would love a second chance with you, Nate. But are you sure about this?"

"Honestly...no, I'm not."

Liberty bristled at his admission, but who could blame him? She had walked away from him once, without much of an explanation. Though she knew that would never happen again, he didn't know that. He didn't know that he was the only man she could ever see herself being happy with.

"But..." he wrapped his arms around her, bubbles tickling her chin, "...I care about you. I'd be lying if I said I didn't have reservations, but we owe it to ourselves to see if there's something still between us. I think there is."

"I won't hurt you again," Liberty said, hoping he could hear and feel the sincerity in her words.

Seconds ticked by before he spoke. "I know you won't. Not intentionally. And I'm going to do my best to treat you like the special woman you are."

Liberty turned slightly to look at him. "You already do."

She moaned against his lips when he kissed her sweetly. Neither of them knew what the future held, but it said a lot about him as a man that he was willing to give her another chance.

Liberty settle back against him.

"Going forward, if you have a problem or are unhappy, you have to tell me. No more keeping everything inside. I can't help if I don't know what's going on."

"I'll try, but I've relied on myself for so long. It might not be easy to always open up and share. I assure you, what happened between us before, will never happen again. I'm older, wiser, and I really do want to make this…you and I, work."

"Earlier at the driving range I talked about you going into law, assuming that was still something you wanted. Was I wrong?"

Liberty had dreamed of being a lawyer for as long as she could remember. Her marriage to Isaac hadn't been ideal, and he was a jerk most of the time, but the first few years he supported her goals. He had even paid for her law degree. Of course it was mostly for selfish reasons, wanting them to be that power couple who dominated the Chicago business world. Liberty bought into the fantasy, and had tried to make the marriage work. Their union wasn't romantic, but they wanted some of the same things. To be successful and they both had wanted a family.

Though Liberty enjoyed the work at the Culpepper's law firm, she didn't like some of the lawyers she supported. Isaac being one of them. She hadn't asked for any special treatment from him, but she had expected to be respected. Isaac belittled her in front of his colleagues and her co-workers. Over the years, that behavior spilled into their home life. With the everyday stresses, she started shutting down emotionally. Then she found out she was pregnant.

Liberty closed her eyes as memories of that time flooded her mind. The baby news shocked her. She and Isaac had been very careful. The plan was for her to take the bar and get her law career going before they started a family. Though she was happy about being pregnant, Isaac made living with him almost unbearable. She had fallen into what she now knew was depression, and had lost the baby at eighteen weeks into her pregnancy.

"Liberty?" Nate kissed her cheek, his arms tightening around her.

Instead of discussing the reasons that hindered her from taking the bar, she said, "I still want to be an attorney. I want to practice law."

"Have you started studying for the bar again?"

She nodded. Liberty hadn't planned to share that bit of information with anyone just in case she didn't pass.

"I had studied and had planned to take the bar, twice, while in Chicago." The test was only given twice a year. The first time she was scheduled to take it, Isaac sabotaged the plan with an overseas trip, insisting she travel with him. He told her he would support her dream of becoming a lawyer. Yet, with his controlling behavior, he always found a way to disrupt her progress.

Nate was silent. Instead of asking what happened, he placed a kiss on the side of her head.

"I'll do whatever I can to support you. I have a feeling you're going to pass this time."

Liberty didn't know what she had done to deserve this man, but she was grateful he was back in her life. "I have a feeling you're right."

Chapter Seventeen

"Are you kidding me? You guys are dating?" Demi stopped, her mouth hanging open. "How? When?"

Demi had asked Liberty to ride to Fairfield with her to tour the potential location for her and Alan's spring wedding. Standing in the ballroom wasn't how Liberty had planned to share the news.

"We were just in the car for forty-five minutes. You didn't think to tell me this during the drive? As a matter of fact, you should've called me right after you two did a little somethin' somethin'. What's wrong with you? You're supposed to tell me everything. Not days later, but within five minutes of all major events. And I'd say, this is pretty major."

Liberty tried not to laugh at the incredulous expression on her sister's pretty face. "First of all, you were out of town on business until yesterday. Secondly, on the ride here, you were telling me about your week, and then the conversation rolled into plans for your wedding. But what difference does it make when I tell you? As long as you know, that's all that really matters."

Demi huffed and glanced around the huge room that was decorated for an event taking place the next day. Since walking in, this was the first time that either of them really took in the beauty of the space.

The color scheme was silver and purple. According to the saleswoman who had been showing them around before she had to go and take a call, the place was set for four hundred guests. All the chairs had silver slip covers and the tables were covered with deep purple table cloths. The elaborate center pieces, flowers and lighting embodied a combination of both colors and seemed to pull the whole space together.

"I love it and the decorations, though I'm not really feeling the colors," Demi whispered. Liberty actually liked them, but that was just her.

"So are we good?" Liberty finally asked.

"We will be once you give me details."

She filled her sister in on the golfing date and all that happened afterward. Not every detail, but enough for her sister to get the gist of what took place leading up to the bathtub conversation.

The past week had been one of the best weeks of Liberty's life. She and Nate had put the finishing touches on the Unity Tower proposal and she had submitted it yesterday. In the evenings, they took turns cooking and ate dinner together. It was turning into a routine Liberty looked forward to throughout the day. Even when they both brought work home, sometimes working in different rooms, their new relationship felt right.

"I can't explain it, Demi. When we're together, it's like we were never apart. All the things I loved about him before are even more pronounced now. He is such a sweet, wonderful, thoughtful man."

"I'll admit, when I met him the other week, I was impressed. Not only was he hotter than you described, I saw the way he looked at you. I also noticed how attuned he was to your needs."

Demi had invited Liberty and Nate to have dinner with her and Alan. Her sister claimed she wanted to thank him for stepping in at the bar. At first, Liberty had debated on asking Nate to attend the small dinner party, but figured all he could say was no. Without hesitation, he accepted the invite. He and Alan had hit it off as if they had known each other for years. Their love for golf and sports in general helped. As for Demi, she hadn't been able to resist Nate's charm.

"My only hesitation when Nate suggested we date and get to know each other again is that I feel so undeserving," Liberty told her sister. "After I—"

"Don't start. It's about time you have some happiness. Though I don't agree with how you ended up with Isaac, I'll be forever grateful for your sacrifices. It's because of you I was able to live in a beautiful home my last few years of high school, with food on the table. And not many college graduates have been able to graduate without student loans. I only wish you would let me pay you back now."

Liberty shook her head. "We've already talked about that. Taking care of your college was an investment in you. I have no regrets about that. I never wanted you to endure the same pressures I felt when I was your age."

"All the more reason why you deserve to be happy. If Nate is willing to forgive and forget and give you guys another chance, you have my blessings. But do you think he has truly forgiven you?"

"He wouldn't have suggested we date if he hadn't. He's not the type of man to play games and he's brutally honest. No, he wouldn't lead me on just to do me wrong."

"Are you sure? What if he's trying to seek revenge? Make you fall in love with him all over again only to dump you soon after. I don't want to see you hurt again."

Liberty would be lying if she said that she wasn't afraid of that possibility. With what she felt for Nate, he had the power to hurt her way more than Isaac ever had.

"I'm sure, Demi," Liberty finally said to her sister. "We're both serious about giving our relationship another try."

"I'm so sorry about the interruption." The sales rep for the venue rushed back into the room. Her gray shoulder-length bob bouncing with every step. The woman was a ball of energy, talking just as fast as she was moving around while she described all that came with renting the room.

Liberty distanced herself from the two women and roamed around the back of the space. She hadn't ever thought about getting married again. Not until now. Not until Nate.

Could she really get that happily-ever-after that she used to dream about when she was younger? She already trusted Nate with her heart and had never stopped loving him. But was she being foolish in thinking that he could leave the past in the past and really forgive her?

Liberty quickly shook the thought free. Her sister was right to be concerned, but Demi didn't know Nate the way she knew him. He wouldn't hurt her.

At least not intentionally.

*

It wasn't often that Nate needed to talk out his thoughts, but this afternoon was another story. He hadn't been able to focus on much of anything for the last two days for worrying about Liberty. She meant so much to him, but he wasn't a hundred percent sure they should be together, especially since she was still in the process of reconstructing her life.

Nate parked in front of his parents' home and headed to the backyard where he knew his father was barbecuing. Not only was the savory aroma filling the air, but the smoke billowing at the back of the house was a sure sign.

"What's up, Dad?" He greeted walking through the gate, closing it behind him.

Lewis glanced up from in front of the grill. "Hey, son. I didn't know you were stopping by today."

Nate climbed the four steps that led to the top of the deck. "Yeah, I was in the neighborhood and figured I'd see if you and Mom were home."

"Well, I'm here, but your mom went to the store." Lewis moved the ribs to the side of the grill and placed some chicken on the rack.

"What's with all of the food?"

"Sarah wanted me to grill enough to get us through a few days. Knowing her, I wouldn't be surprised if she expected you and Nick to stop by."

Nate smiled. They used to joke that Sarah Jenkins-Moore was psychic when it came to her boys. She might not have been their birth mother, but she had a sixth sense where he and Nick were concerned. Nate would never forget the time when she paced the floor one night. He and Nick were around sixteen. Nick had gone out with some friends and hours after he'd left, their mom claimed that something was wrong.

They hadn't been able to reach his brother and the anxiousness rolling off of Sarah could be felt throughout the house. An hour later they'd gotten a call saying that Nick had been in an accident. He only suffered a broken arm, but none of them ever doubted her intuition again.

She was an amazing mom and the only mother he and Nick had ever known. Their biological father had died in the military before they were born. Then their birth mother, Natalie, died of kidney failure making Nate and Nick orphans at the age of one. Natalie and Sarah had been cousins, as well as best friends. As their godmother, Sarah stepped in and adopted them.

Nate would be forever grateful to her. It hadn't been easy being a single mom, especially with twin boys. But all of their lives changed when Lewis came onto the scene when Nate was three. He married Sarah and adopted him and Nick shortly after. From day one Lewis had treated them like his own, teaching them everything they needed to know about being a man. What Nate respected the most about Lewis was the way he treated Sarah. Her happiness and security were his top priority, and he worshiped the ground she walked on. Nate planned to treat his own wife the same should he ever get married.

"What's on your mind son?" Lewis pulled a couple of beers out of the small refrigerator near the grill. He handed one to Nate and then joined him at the table.

"Thanks." Nate took a long drag from his beer before placing it on the table. They sat in silence for the longest time, and Nate stared out over the manicured lawn. His mother's flower garden was fully bloomed and it looked as if she'd added some new plants.

"I know you didn't come over here to admire your mother's handy work with the yard. Does this unexpected visit and your silence have anything to do with Liberty?"

Nate grunted. Maybe mothers weren't the only ones with a sixth sense. Nate had come to talk, but at the moment he wasn't sure what he wanted to share. Lewis knew about Liberty's return, but not about them getting back together. Nate filled him in on the last couple of months.

"Sounds like you two have been spending a lot of time together. Are you having second thoughts?" Lewis asked.

"No. Not exactly." Nate pushed his chair back and leaned forward, his elbows on his thighs and his fingers steepled. "Man, Dad. Liberty used to be everything I ever wanted in a woman. Heck, everything I wanted in a wife. She was gorgeous. Selfless. Confident. Independent. I even liked that she was a little stubborn."

Lewis chuckled. "Was she as stubborn as your mother?" Sarah was headstrong like the rest of the Jenkins women, tenacious, and used to getting her way.

Nate laughed. "Maybe not as stubborn as Mom, but close."

"You said Liberty *was* once all of those things. I take it that's changed."

"She still has *some* of those qualities, but she's…I don't know, different. Not just her name has changed. I know she's been through a lot, and pulling her life back together hasn't been easy. But she's not as confident as she used to be, and there's still a sadness about her. That jerk she was married to broke her spirit, and I don't know if she can get that back."

Every day that Nate and Liberty spent together, she shared bits and pieces about her marriage. Explaining how unhappy she was and how the relationship had deteriorated over the years. Last night she talked more about her time at the Culpepper's law firm. Isaac had been emotionally abusive toward her at work and at home. Liberty knew she had to find a way out of the marriage, but it wasn't until he hit her that she finally left.

"I think Liberty is keeping something from me," Nate said. "Something she thinks will make me have second thoughts about her and me."

"How do you know? Has she hinted to something being wrong?"

"Not really, but... I just have this feeling that I can't shake."

"Now you're sounding like your mother. She has more *feelings* than anyone I know."

Nate grinned. "And she's usually right."

"That's true," Lewis said nodding.

"With Liberty, I've been mainly trying to show her that she can trust me. That she can confide in me. Don't get me wrong, we have good communication, but I think she's still unsure about our relationship. She's even mentioned that she doesn't trust her own judgment, and to me, sometimes it feels like she's waiting for me to hurt her. To treat her wrong or get back at her for what happened in the past."

"Is that your intent? Are you still holding some animosity toward her?"

Nate shook his head. "No. I really do care about her. I want to see where this relationship goes. She's special, but if she doesn't believe that of herself, there's nothing I can say or do to change her mind."

"Maybe not, but being with you might help. Think about it. Can you imagine being around someone for years who always put you down, made you feel like you're unworthy, and have you questioning your own abilities? That girl sounds like a survivor. Some women never get over the type of stress and hurt she endured. Has Liberty gone through any type of therapy?"

"She went through therapy while she was going through her divorce. I might just be reading more into what she's saying and not saying than necessary. I guess I want the old Kayla back."

"Well, you might as well give that idea up. She's not the same person and neither are you. Besides, it's clear you two didn't know each other as well as you once thought you did."

"Yeah, you're right."

"If you're as serious about her as I think you are, take your time and get to know Liberty. Be gentle with her. Show her how a woman should really be treated."

That's exactly what Nate was doing, or at least trying to do. Liberty was such a sweetheart. There were times that he just wanted to hold her tight and never let her go. He never wanted to see her hurt again.

"But Nate, if this young lady is fragile, don't start something you don't plan on finishing."

"I want Liberty in my life for as long as she'll have me. I knew the first day I met her that she was the one for me."

Nate also knew she was the reason he hadn't been able to open his heart to another woman. He couldn't explain the connection between them. She held a special spot in his heart that no other had ever been able to fill. He might've been concerned about her emotional state, but there was no doubt in his mind that he still loved her.

Perhaps his father was right. Maybe loving on Liberty was all she needed to regain confidence in herself, and to know that she was worthy of love.

"So, when are we going to meet this young lady?"

"I'm thinking about bringing her to Sunday brunch next week."

"Wow. You must be real serious about her if you're planning to subject her to the Jenkins clan." Lewis laughed and Nate joined in.

"Yeah, hopefully they don't scare her away."

Chapter Eighteen

Liberty was a nervous wreck. She barely slept the night before in anticipation of meeting Nate's parents. But meeting the whole family at the infamous Sunday brunch added a whole different wave of anxiousness.

She had heard of immediate family members eating together on occasion, but cousins, uncles, and aunts hooking up every week? Who did that? Apparently, the Jenkins family. Nate mentioned that it was a tradition started many years ago, and forty-plus years later, it was still going strong. And if any of the grandkids didn't show up, their grandmother, Katherine, would personally call the following Monday to find out why.

Liberty stared out the passenger side window of Nate's car as the city went by in a blur. Had he told them about why she broke things off with him in college? What if they didn't like her? What if they didn't think she was good enough for Nate? Would they be out for blood for breaking his heart? Imagining the possibilities made her nauseous.

Nate reached over and grabbed hold of her hand, giving it a slight squeeze. "Relax. I can feel how tense you are all the way over here. You have nothing to worry about. My family is going to love you. I promise."

Nate held on to her hand until they reached Indian Hill, a Cincinnati suburb. Every house seemed bigger than the next as they drove through his grandparents' neighborhood. Liberty knew the Jenkins family had done well for themselves, but she had no idea his grandparents lived in a mansion.

Seeing the huge homes reminded her of the first time Isaac had taken her to his parents' estate. He'd been trying to impress her with what they had. It took her a while to realize that they might've been wealthy, but they were horrible human beings. Quick to belittle anyone who wasn't in the same tax bracket as them. Liberty hoped Nate's family wasn't like that.

"I might not be ready for this," she said once he parked near the end of the double-wide, circular driveway. There were cars everywhere.

He looked at her, concern radiating in his dark eyes. "Baby, I'm not going to force you to do anything, but I'd like for you to meet my family. What are you afraid of?"

Liberty looked back at the home before returning her attention to him. "Seeing their estate reminds me of the times that Isaac took me to his parents' home. It was never a good experience, and I always felt like an outsider. What if your family hates me for the choices I made in college?"

Nate turned to face her, his arm on the back of the seat. "I hope you're not comparing me to Isaac or my family to his family. I can assure you we are not the same people. I will warn you, though. My family is nosy, loud, and opinionated. Some of them are a pain in the ass, but they won't disrespect you. And what happened between you and me in the past, that's none of their business. If anyone says anything inappropriately to you, let me know."

Some of the tension eased from her body. If the Jenkins family was anything like Nate, she had nothing to worry about.

"If at any time you want to leave, tell me and we're out. All right?"

146

"Okay."

He exited the car and walked around to the passenger side and opened her door.

"Looks like you'll get to meet my cousin Peyton and her family first," Nate said as he helped Liberty out of the car. He nodded toward the woman walking toward them with a handsome man, a baby, and a little girl trailing a short distance behind.

"Is she the one who used to manage Jenkins & Sons but now lives in New York? The one married to the private investigator?"

"Yes. That's her. They arrived in town this morning."

The night before, Nate had given Liberty some insight into many of the people she would meet at the brunch. Seemed the family was dominated with mostly men, but Nate spoke highly of his female cousins. All of them were either construction workers or had worked in the trades at one time. Peyton was an electrician by trade, and did side-jobs in New York, but mainly was a stay at home mom.

"What's up, stranger?" Nate said, hugging Peyton.

"Not much. It's good seeing you," Peyton said before pulling away from Nate and extending her hand. "You must be Liberty."

"Liberty, this is my cousin, Peyton, her husband Michael, and their children."

"It's a pleasure to meet you all," Liberty said, comforted by their friendliness.

Peyton's husband, Michael, carried their one-year-old son, while their daughter held on to Peyton's hand. Had Nate not mentioned it, Liberty wouldn't have known that the little girl, Michaela, was actually Peyton's stepdaughter. They looked so much alike.

Liberty smiled up at Nate when he grabbed her hand. They fell in step behind Peyton and her family as they all headed up the long driveway toward the house.

"That little guy is getting big," Nate said of Michael Jr.

"Yeah, man, he definitely has the Jenkins family appetite," Michael said over his shoulder.

Peyton laughed and nudged her husband in the arm. "Don't be talking about my greedy family."

"Liberty, you'll see. Greedy is an understatement. This family is always eating." Michael laughed, dodging a swat from his wife.

They all laughed, and the nerves Liberty had been battling with earlier subsided.

The smell of barbecue, loud talking, laughing, and music greeted them as they drew closer to the backyard. Nate had mentioned that during the summer months, many of them lounged outside, played volleyball, horseshoes and turned the brunch into a family picnic. Now it was officially fall, and the temperature had dropped to the low-seventies. The sun was shining brightly, and it was still a perfect day for outdoor activities.

When they approached the six-foot wood fence, Liberty slowed and squeezed Nate's hand. It had been a long time since she met a boyfriend's family.

He lowered his head and kissed her, pushing away even more of her anxiety. "It's going to be fine. I promise."

"I know. I was just being silly worrying for no reason."

He had been so patient with her over the past month. It was going to take time for her to get used to a kind man who respected her. How sad was that? She couldn't believe she had gotten used to how poorly Isaac and his family treated her.

The moment they entered the yard that looked more like a small park, Liberty felt at home. Small groups of people were scattered everywhere seeming to be enjoying themselves. Some hung out near the grill on the patio, while others were at picnic tables or sitting by the in-ground swimming pool. If she thought the front of the home was impressive, the backyard was an event planner's dream. She had expected a lot of people, but the fifty-plus exceeded her expectations, and that was just outside.

The next few minutes included a whirlwind of introductions. There was no way she would remember all of the names and the relationship to Nate. Liberty could understand why the grandmother insisted on the family coming together. The positive energy floating around the large group was palpable.

"Nate, you made it," a man said coming out of the house, a beer in one hand and a plate in the other.

"Yep, we just got here. Liberty, this is my uncle, Ben. Uncle Ben, this is Liberty," Nate introduced proudly.

"You're even more beautiful than Nate described. It's nice to finally meet you."

Liberty smiled. "It's a pleasure to meet you as well. Nate talks about you all the time." Liberty had heard so much about him, she felt like she already knew him. Taking in the tall, handsome man with mesmerizing eyes had her wondering what the hell type of gene pool they had going on. She hadn't seen so many gorgeous people in one spot in a long time. Nate had mentioned that Ben was his mother's youngest brother and only about fourteen years older than Nate. That would put him at around fifty, but he didn't look that much older than Nate. The saying, *black don't crack*, definitely applied to the Jenkins family.

"Well, as long as whatever he said was good, then you can believe him."

"It was very good."

They talked to him a few more minutes and she was surprised that Nate had told him she was studying for the bar. She was filled with gratitude when Ben told her if she had any questions or if there was anything he could do to help, just give him a call.

When they approached the back deck, she saw a few familiar faces.

"What's up you two?" Liam said giving Nate a fist bump before bending down and kissing her on her cheek. "Welcome to brunch, Liberty. You're a brave woman coming to hang out with all of these animals." He grinned and she laughed.

Nate wrapped his arm around her waist and started pointing at people. "That's my cousin, Jerry." He pointed to a tall, very muscular, dark-skinned man.

"Nice to meet you. I've heard a lot about you," he said shaking her hand and flashing a devilish smile that she was sure had women throwing themselves at him.

"This is my cousin, Ben Junior, Uncle Ben's youngest son," Nate said of the man who was a little shorter than Jerry and had light brown eyes. "Have you guys seen my parents?"

Jerry pointed to the door with his thumb. "Inside."

Holding her hand again, Nate escorted Liberty into the house, giving more introductions while showing her around the grand space. They kept moving until they reached the kitchen where Nate introduced her to his grandmother, some of his aunts and cousins.

"Gram, have you seen my mom?" Nate asked just as a woman who looked like a younger version of his grandmother walked in. She had smooth skin the color of milk chocolate, and was short with rounded hips. She zoned in on her son.

"Hey, sweetheart. I was wondering when you would get here," she said accepting a kiss on the cheek from Nate, but her gaze was on Liberty.

"Mom, this is Liberty. Liberty, this is my mother, Sarah Moore."

"Hey, young lady. It's a pleasure to finally meet you."

Liberty wasn't sure what she had expected, but when Sarah hugged her like only a mother could, Liberty didn't want her to let go. She felt such warmth from the gesture that all of her inhibitions about whether the family would dislike her flew out the door.

Nate winked at Liberty and mouthed, *I told you.*

*

"All right, I'm ready for my niece," Nate said, an hour later, when he walked into the nursery. His cousin, Martina, had set it up in one of the second-floor bedrooms at their grandparents' home. Nick was in there changing his daughter's diaper.

"I can't remember the last time I saw you this happy," Nick said, as he fixed Chanelle's clothes and then handed her to Nate.

"What are you talking about?" Nate asked, planting kisses against the baby's cheek and neck, eliciting a toothless grin from her. She was growing too fast. Soon she'd be crawling and getting into everything. "Chanelle, tell your daddy that I'm always happy."

"Not like lately." Nick washed his hands in the sink near the changing table. "I can't help but wonder if a cute little project manager has anything to do with that constant grin you've been wearing."

"Maybe."

"You know what this means don't you?" Nick asked, drying his hands.

"No, but I'm sure you're going to tell me."

"If you end up walking down the aisle with the proposal queen, you'll have me to thank."

Nate frowned. "How do you figure that?"

"If it weren't for me, you wouldn't have agreed to do the proposal. And if we hadn't gotten involved with LCA, you never would've run into your college sweetheart."

"You don't know that. I could've run into her at the movies or the grocery store. Quit trying to take credit for my good fortune."

Nick laughed. "You ungrateful a—"

"Don't be cursing around my goddaughter. She has delicate ears." At that moment, Chanelle flashed a bright smile as if she understood Nate was talking about her. "God, she has to be the cutest kid alive."

"She definitely is, and I can't wait to have a ton more just like her." Nick placed a kiss on top of her curly head. "Have you and Liberty talked about kids?"

"Nope. It's too soon for all of that." Despite his words, Nate knew in his heart, he had found the woman he wanted to spend the rest of his life with. It was only a matter of time before they started talking marriage. "We're still getting to know each other," he said to his brother.

"Maybe, but you might want to give her a heads up about you wanting six children. Women need advanced notice if you're expecting them to have that many kids."

Nate laughed. He would love to have a house full of kids, and he'd be lying if he said he hadn't been thinking about that idea more. Not since college did he wonder what it would be like to procreate with Liberty.

"Speaking of Liberty, let me go find her. I'm taking Chanelle with me."

"Fine with me. If she starts fussing, I'll be in the theater room, but you can take her to Sumeera. She's in the kitchen…I think."

When they arrived on the first floor, they ran into their grandfather's cousin, Dexter.

"What's up, Dex?" Nick and Nate greeted the older man, each shaking his hand. Dexter, a former army ranger and construction worker, had run into some trouble a few years ago. It took him time to get his life back together, and lately he had started spending more time with family.

"I'm glad I ran into you guys. Follow me," Dexter said. Nate and Nick gave each other a curious glance and let Dexter lead them toward an all-season room on the side of the house.

Before heading down the short hallway that led to the room, Dexter stopped and stepped to the side. They could see the people in the room without being spotted.

"See the woman sitting next to your mother? The one with the red highlights in her hair and almond-shaped eyes, and pretty lips. Who is she?"

Nate and Nick exchanged a look and laughed at the description.

"Who, my mother-in-law?" Nick asked.

The interest in Dexter's eyes couldn't be missed. He had good taste. Mona was a nice-looking woman, but Nick's mother-in-law had recently moved to Cincinnati after walking away from a long-term relationship. Nate would be surprised if she was interested in getting into another relationship right away.

"Introduce me," Dexter said to Nick, pushing him toward the room.

"I'll catch you guys later." Nate headed in the opposite direction. "Alright, baby girl. Let's go find *my* woman."

Chapter Nineteen

Liberty sat in the oversized sitting room with some of the women in the family. She couldn't remember the last time she'd eaten so much. Considering the family were big meat eaters, Liberty had been pleasantly surprised that they had prepared a number of dishes that she could eat. Everything from grilled vegetables, Thai rice noodle salad, to Liberty's new favorite dish, stuffed peppers.

"Did you have enough to eat?" Christina asked. Wearing an off-the-shoulder, white, hippie-style dress with a floral wreath headband, Christina looked very much the free-spirited, flower-child Nate had described.

"I did. Thank you. Everything was excellent. I don't think I've ever eaten this much in my life."

Peyton walked in at that moment carrying her son on her hip. "Isn't it scary to know that this family eats like this every week?"

Liberty laughed. "That is interesting, but you all look great. I'd be a thousand pounds if I ate like this weekly."

"The secret is, we only eat like this on Sundays. The rest of the week, we stuff ourselves with salad and water," Toni added and sat next to Liberty on the sofa. Today she wore a T-shirt that said *Stay Calm, Master Plumber in the House.*

"Dang, this family is being overrun by kids. They're everywhere." Martina scooped up her daughter who had fallen asleep on a mound of pillows. "Soon we're going to have to get a few nannies to help with them during Sunday brunch."

"There will be no nannies in my house," Katherine Jenkins said from a chair near the windows. She stood and headed to the door. "I had seven kids. Me and your grandfather took care of them by ourselves."

"Yeah, and look how they turned out." Martina ducked when Katherine swatted at her while others in the room laughed.

They left, but others hung around. When Liberty and Nate first arrived, Nate stuck by her until one of his aunts assured him they'd keep her company. Once he was sure she was okay with that, Nate had made a hasty retreat. He told her he'd be in the lower level watching football if she needed him.

"You look lost without Zack Junior," Christina said to Jada who was sitting in an overstuff chair near the other end of the sofa.

It didn't take long for Liberty to identify the pretty, petite woman. Dressed in a stylish, floral sundress with red-bottom high-heeled sandals, Jada was perfectly made up with every hair in place. Hard to believe the fashionista was once a sheet metal worker. She had quit her job after marrying her husband, a former NFL running back.

"Little Zack is hanging out with his father," Jada said, sitting with one leg crossed over the other, her sandal dangling from her foot.

Just then, her hunk of a husband walked in carrying the curly-headed three-month old in the crook of his arm as if the baby weighed nothing.

A stab of loss pierced Liberty in the heart. At thirty-four, she thought she'd be married to the love of her life with at least three children by now. But the moment she married Isaac, she knew that wouldn't be the case. At least the love of her life part. It was when she'd gotten pregnant that she thought at least she'd have a child of her own to love.

"You changed his clothes?" Jada shrieked, catching Liberty's attention. "What happened to his suit and his dress shoes?"

Earlier, the baby looked as if he'd just returned from church, though that hadn't been the case according to Christina. According to her, not only did Jada keep the baby in the finest clothes, she dressed him up as if he was a miniature business man. Liberty had thought that funny. Now the baby was wearing a T-shirt, jeans, and the smallest Timberland boots Liberty had ever seen.

"He was tired of the suit," Zack said, his lips twitching as if trying to hold back a grin. Everyone else in the room was rolling laughing, except for Jada.

"I think you need psychiatric help," Toni said to Jada while still laughing. "He's a baby, not some CEO or baby doll. You're the only person in the world who changes their child's clothes three or four times a day for no reason at all."

"And if that's not enough, she has a diaper bag, bottles, pacifiers, and bibs to match every single outfit," Christina said to Liberty and smirked.

Wow, Liberty thought. That did seem a bit excessive.

"You guys need to mind your own business," Jada grumbled, but her facial expression changed when Zack put the baby in her arms. Liberty didn't miss the love radiating in her eyes as she held her son. The little boy was a looker with tanned skinned, a combination of his African American mother and Caucasian father's skin tone.

"Alright, leave my wife alone." Zack bent down and kissed Jada lips. If she was mad at him, it didn't show when she smiled and cupped her hand over his scruff-covered cheek.

Another stab of pain hit Liberty in the heart, and she diverted her gaze. All afternoon she'd been subjected to watching happily married couples who had the cutest kids. Even though she and Nate's relationship was progressing nicely, she wondered if she would ever have anything close to what she was witnessing.

Having endured the loving couples and adorable baby moments all afternoon, Liberty didn't know how much more she could take. Though being surrounded by people who clearly loved each other, even with the good-natured teasing, was refreshing. That hadn't been the case with Isaac's family. Toward the end of their marriage, Liberty hadn't even bothered attending family functions. Not wanting to endure the constant criticizing or witnessing the holier-than-thou attitudes.

One by one the cousins started filing out of the room, only leaving Christina and Toni, who were standing near the windows discussing a project their grandmother wanted them to handle.

Liberty thought about going in search of Nate. Before she could stand, he stopped outside the entrance to the room, talking to a man whose name Liberty couldn't remember.

Her heart swelled as she watched him cradle his niece. He was a natural. The love for her could easily be seen each time he stared down at the baby. If she and Nate ever discussed marriage, what would he think about her not wanting to try having another baby? Would he dump her?

"Hey there." He sat on the sofa next to her and wrapped his free arm around her shoulder before he kissed her lips.

"Hey yourself." She glanced down at the baby who had her tiny fist in her mouth as she stared up at Liberty. Dressed in an adorable pink dress with matching socks, Chanelle could easily be a pint-sized model for everything cute and frilly.

"Do you want to hold her?"

"Um, no. That's okay. Besides, she seems very content in her uncle's arms." Liberty tried to smile.

Nate lowered his voice. "What's wrong? Are you feeling okay?"

Perceptive as ever. Her first instinct was to say no, but she didn't want to be the cause of them leaving the brunch early.

"I'm fine." She glanced at the baby again and Liberty's heart squeezed. Suddenly needing some air, it took everything within her not to get up and leave the room.

When Chanelle started to fuss, Nate lifted her against his chest and spoke softly, rocking her gently.

Liberty's heart squeezed a little more. Their gazes met and held for a second before he narrowed his eyes.

"You sure you don't want to hold her? You have a longing look in your—"

"I said no," she blurted harsher than intended and wanted to kick herself when Nate raised an eyebrow. She didn't dare look over at Christina and Toni.

"CJ, can you and Toni give us some privacy?"

"Sure."

"Here, take Chanelle to Sumeera."

Nate handed off the baby and then waited until they closed the door before he turned back to Liberty.

"You don't like kids?"

"I love kids," Liberty said quietly.

"Then why are—"

"Can't you just drop it, Nate?" She started to move away, but he was quicker. With his long arm snaked around her waist, he pulled her close.

"I know something's wrong. I hope you know you can talk to me about anything." He placed a kiss on the side of her head. It was just as sensual as if he had kissed her lips.

Liberty felt like crap. Why did he have to be so sweet? How would she ever be able to tell him that though she loved kids, she would never try to have any again? A woman could only take so much disappointment. She'd had enough sorrow in her world to last a lifetime.

"Talk to me."

"I don't know, Nate. While we're hanging out with your family might not be the best time to talk about this."

"If something is bothering you, then this is the perfect time. Besides, it's just you and me here."

Liberty feared his reaction. She didn't want to lose him.

"Tell me what's wrong." He held her hand, and that should have brought her comfort, but instead her anxiety increased.

Just tell him.

"Weeks ago, when we decided to give our relationship a second chance, you said no more secrets."

His face clouded with unease and uncertainty built within her as seconds ticked by. She should've brought this up in conversation long before, especially since she knew how much he wanted a family. But at the time she hadn't been sure they'd be able to rebuild their relationship.

"There's something I didn't tell you. I guess I wasn't really sure how."

"Just tell me, Liberty," he said, an edge to his tone.

"Five years ago, when I was studying for the bar...I got pregnant." His hand on hers went slack, but he didn't release her.

"You...you have a child?" he asked confused. His dark eyes showing disbelief. "Where—"

"I miscarried at four and half months."

"Oh, man. Baby, I'm sorry." He wrapped his arms around her and they sat back on the sofa. "I guess seeing all of the babies here today hasn't been easy."

"I had wanted a family, but had been resigned to the fact that it wouldn't happen since I had married Isaac. He knew I didn't love him, but since I agreed to marry him..."

"Was having a child part of the contract?"

Liberty nodded. "He wanted an heir. And to be honest, I wanted a baby. I tried to make the relationship work, especially early in our marriage. But according to Isaac, I couldn't do anything right." She paused. "I froze whenever he touched me, and I'm not just talking about intimately. I barely wanted him to look at me. He and I both knew why. I didn't love him. I couldn't fake that no matter how hard I tried."

It had been emotionally painful to be with Isaac when her heart belonged to someone else. Even though Liberty thought she would never see Nate again, he was never far from her thoughts. Never far from her heart.

"We hadn't planned to have a child until after I started my career. But since I hadn't taken the bar, the timeline of starting a family kept getting pushed back. I eventually realized Isaac didn't care about my career and couldn't care less if I took the bar. But he did want a child.

"I allowed him and that stupid contract to control my life. I was so unhappy, Nate. In every aspect of my life. I felt like a complete failure. Even so, I tried to make the best of every situation. Isaac had helped my family, I owed him. I tried to be the dutiful wife by catering to his needs, accompanying him to events, smiling, when what I really wanted to do was cry. On the outside looking in, we probably looked like the ideal couple.

"Needless to say, I was shocked when I got pregnant since we used protection, and I had mixed feelings. We had been married almost eight years. The thought of bringing a child into a loveless marriage haunted me to the point of sleepless nights and barely eating. But I wanted that baby so bad. I wanted someone to love."

"Did your ex start treating you better once he found out you were pregnant?"

"He did for the first couple of months, but then one of their businesses lost a million-dollar contract, and his family blamed him. He blamed me. Isaac made my life a living hell. Our already dysfunctional relationship got worse when he reneged on part of the contract that involved my parents.

"What do you mean?"

"My father worked at a manufacturing company owned by the Culpeppers, and suddenly, his hours were cut in half. He struggled to pay rent on the house that Isaac owned. The deal had been that if my parents paid the rent on time each month, after ten years, Isaac would sign the title of the house over to me. I never told my parents about the contract."

"So even after all those years, they never knew why you married Isaac or the requirement about the rent?"

Liberty shook her head. "The contract stipulated that I couldn't tell anyone the details of our marriage. Besides, I never wanted them to know the real reason I married Isaac. It would've broken their hearts, and they would've insisted I break the contract no matter what would've happened to them.

"My father had picked up a part-time job, and my mother worked as a seamstress. It wasn't enough. By the time I found out they had fallen behind on the rent, Isaac had put the house on the market. I knew he wouldn't sell the house to me, so I gifted the money I had saved from working at the law firm to my sister. She financed the balance and purchased the home. All of this went on while I was studying for the bar. I was tired, stressed, and just…miserable. Not a good combination at any given time, but especially when you're pregnant."

"And you lost the baby."

Liberty nodded. "Two days before I was supposed to take the bar."

"Ah, man."

"I was in a bad place, Nate." She shook her head thinking about how she had mentally and emotionally shut down. She had stayed in bed for months, not caring about her job, life, or anything else.

"What did Isaac say about all of this?"

"By this time in our marriage, Isaac didn't give a damn about me, and I wanted nothing to do with him. We stayed in separate rooms and we barely saw each other. I never cared to find out for sure, but I'm almost positive he was cheating on me. Yet, he refused to give me a divorce. He said I had embarrassed him enough. He wouldn't let me embarrass him more by walking away from our marriage.

"At that point, I stopped caring about almost everything. I figured I'd ride out the contract which included me getting enough money to start my life over after twenty years with him, but..." She shrugged. "You already know the rest."

Nate removed his arm from around Liberty and sat forward, his elbows resting on his thighs. He must have thought her a total loser. Hearing herself share this part of her life, made her realize just how lost she had been back then. There were some moments when it seemed like she was an observer of her life. Not the person who had actually experienced that type of drama.

Liberty glanced at Nate's back wishing he would say something.

"Nate!" Someone yelled from the hallway, sounding as if they were walking past the room. The door was closed and Liberty wasn't sure who the voice belonged to.

Nate stood and headed for the door, but stopped as if remembering she was still there. "Um," he said, rubbing a hand over his head and looking as if he wasn't sure what to say.

She inhaled a breath and rose slowly from the sofa, anticipation squeezing her lungs as she awaited his response.

"Nate!" That same unknown person yelled again in the distance.

Nate reached for her hand. "Come on. Let me see what's going on out there."

Liberty released the anxious breath she hadn't realized she'd still been holding. She allowed him to lead her out of the room, concerned that he still hadn't responded to her.

They went to the kitchen where a few people were sitting at the table eating and others were discussing storing leftovers.

"Who was calling me?" Nate asked his mother and Christina who were standing at the counter putting food into storage containers.

"I'm not sure, but I think it was Aunt Mary," Christina said. She didn't look up from the Tupperware dish she was covering, and Liberty wondered where they planned to put all the food that was left.

Needing something to do, she pulled away from Nate and rinsed her hands in the sink. "What can I do to help?" she asked.

"Babe, you don't have to help. I'm one of the ones on kitchen duty today. We can handle it," Nate said, sidling up next to her.

"It's the least I can do since I made a pig of myself."

Sarah chuckled. "Girl, if everyone thought like you, Momma wouldn't have a clean-up schedule hanging on the pantry door." She nodded to the closed door that was near the refrigerator.

"Yeah, now that the guys have been added to the rotation, Gram has to practically threaten their lives to get them to do dishes," Christina added.

Nate grunted. "We're not that bad."

Sarah bumped him with her hip. "You're not that bad, but your brother and cousins act as if they're too good to do dishes. Why else would Jerry try to talk your grandmother into letting him put an industrial size dishwasher in here?"

Martina walked into the kitchen loaded down with more empty dishes and Liberty hurried across the room to take some of them from her.

"Whew! Thank you. Good I didn't drop anything. Otherwise, Gram would have my head."

Liberty started spooning up leftover potato salad into a container that could fit into the refrigerator.

"Where the heck is Nate?" Mary called out from the hallway before walking into the kitchen. "Boy, haven't you heard me calling your name? There's a lady here to see you. I found her outside at the front door."

Her? Liberty stiffened, bracing herself. Nate had told her that he had never invited a woman to Sunday brunch before.

"Who is it?" he questioned. He patted Liberty's hip and kissed her on the cheek before heading to the door. He hadn't taken two steps when a gorgeous woman dressed in all white floated into the kitchen.

"Hey, Nate. I was hoping you'd be here." The woman hurried to him, smiling brightly and reached up to kiss him, but he leaned away before she made contact.

Nate stood rigid. His jaw clenched with an unyielding look in his eyes. It was the same silent anger Liberty had experienced that first day in J & S's conference room. She didn't know the woman, but the tension radiating off of Nate was a sure sign he wasn't happy to see her.

"What the hell are you doing here?" he growled through gritted teeth, gripping the woman at the elbow and quickly escorting her out of the kitchen.

"Oh this should be interesting," Martina said, humor in her voice.

"Don't start MJ," Sarah warned.

"Hey, I'm just sayin'. He's never brought a woman to brunch, and today he has two here. It's about damn time we had a little excitement around here," she cracked and strolled out of the kitchen.

Christina, who stood next to Liberty, patted her hand. "Ignore her. She's lacking tact, and on most days good common sense."

Liberty tried to smile, but couldn't stop the worry settling into her bones. Only moments ago, she had bared her soul to Nate, telling him about the baby she had lost, but thought about daily. She had no idea what he thought of her admission. Now he was with a gorgeous woman discussing God knows what while she wondered if she had just ruined her second chance with him.

Chapter Twenty

Nate didn't release Angel until they reached the side of the house. There hadn't been many places he could take her where they wouldn't have an audience. "What the hell are you doing here?"

"I wanted us to talk, but you've been avoiding my calls. I went to your house and when I realized you weren't there, I figured you'd be here."

Unease swept through Nate as he stared at her. Something was definitely wrong with this woman, and for the first time he was afraid that she was capable of anything.

"What do you mean you went to my house?" He rarely invited women to his home, especially when the relationship was new. "How do you even know where I live or where my grandparents live?" Nate asked Angel.

"I looked up the addresses. I really wanted to see you and you mentioned once that you usually eat at your grandparents' house on Sundays." She shrugged as if it was no big deal. "I figured—"

"Angel, I was very clear when I told you that I didn't want to see you anymore." Nate got in her face having a hard time keeping his anger at bay. "Why is that so hard for you to understand?"

She took a step back and placed her hands on her hips. "We had something special, Nate. You can't just lead me on and then toss me away."

"Dammit, Angel! What is wrong with you? I've been telling you this for a couple of months now. If I had changed my mind, I would have called you. Hell, I would have returned some of your calls!"

"I am so sick of guys like you! You treat women real sweet with the thoughtful dates, fancy dinners, and flower deliveries. Make them fall for you and then bam! It's over!"

"I never sent you flowers!"

"Damn you, Nate! I have feelings!" She pounded on his chest with closed fists until he grabbed her wrists, but quickly released her when she tried pulling away.

"I don't know what your problem is, but don't you *ever* touch me again," Nate ground out.

"Everything all right out here?"

Angel startled and whirled around. Nate had already spotted the two men behind Angel just before she started hitting him. Toni's husband, Craig, and Ben stood near the front of the house a few feet away. If Nate wasn't so pissed, he would laugh. A former cop and a lawyer. What did they think he would do to the woman? Then again, maybe it was good they were there. He was mad enough to do something stupid, like threaten to strangle her if she ever stepped to him again.

"Everything is fine," Nate said, glad they didn't move from their spot. He needed witnesses if Angel did anything crazy.

When she returned her attention to him, Nate said, "I never sent you flowers, and I never led you on. I'm sorry if you thought my kindness meant more than what it was, kindness. But I've been up front with you from the beginning regarding my feelings."

She narrowed her eyes at him. "Does this have anything to do with that woman I've been seeing you with?"

Fear like nothing Nate had ever felt clawed up his spine. He didn't know if she was baiting him, or if she'd been following him. "What woman?"

"You know what woman!" she snarled. "The bitch I've seen coming and going from your house."

Oh hell no.

"You've been watching me?" he ground out, shock by her admission.

She seemed to realize what she'd said and started back peddling. "I was in your neighborhood one day and saw you walking a lady to her car. I wondered…"

If this crazy woman was keeping tabs on him, he and Liberty could be in danger.

Nate waved Craig and Ben over, and Angel glanced over her shoulder at them.

"Angel, I want you to meet a couple of people."

"This is my cousin, Detective Craig Logan," Nate said even though Craig had resigned from the police force to start a security consulting business. "And this is my uncle, Attorney Ben Jenkins."

She greeted them with a slow nod probably wondering why they were the only ones out there and why he was introducing them. It was time he nipped this nightmare in the bud.

"Is there a problem here?" Craig asked. No doubt he picked up on Nate describing him as a detective and knew something wasn't right.

"What do I need to do to make Angel understand that though I think she's a nice enough woman, I'm not interested? What do you suggest, Craig? She's stalking me, and she just hit me. How do I get a restraining order against her?"

Angel gasped. "I am not stalking you!"

"What would you call showing up at my house, following me, and then coming here to my grandparents' home? If that wasn't enough, you assaulted me." He pointed at his chest where she had hit him. "I've told you more than once that whatever you and I had was finished."

"Ma'am is this true?" Craig asked, his deep authoritative voice added to the stern look on his face. When he was a cop, Craig had been a badass. Nate had witnessed him in action during a couple of situations that Toni had gotten wrapped up in.

Angel shook her head. "No. No, there's been a misunderstanding. I—I…"

"Tell you what. You leave now, refrain from contacting Nate, and I'm sure he won't pursue charges against you. I'll walk you to your car."

"Nate, I'm—"

"Goodbye, Angel." Nate needed to get back inside. He could only imagine what Liberty must have been thinking. First, she shares a very personal story about herself, and he hadn't had a chance to respond. Hell, he actually hadn't known what to say. And then a strange woman storms into the kitchen and almost kisses him.

But the untimely interruption gave him time to think. If he ever expected to have a life with Liberty, he had to once and for all leave the past in the past. He had to somehow block out the fact that she had married and gotten pregnant by an asshole. Not even hypnosis would be able to wipe away the visual of Isaac's hands anywhere on her body. But if Nate didn't let the past go, he and Liberty wouldn't be able to move forward.

Listening to her recount how she had lost her baby and her dream of becoming a lawyer at the same time, was like a punch in the chest. She was one of the sweetest, most deserving people he knew. No one should have to endure all that she'd been through. She needed some happiness in her life, and he was just the man to give it to her.

"I guess that Jenkins' charm is as potent as ever," Ben said, clapping Nate on the shoulder before they reached the front door. "You know, I'd expect one of Jerry's women to show up here, but you…I'm surprised."

"I'm telling you, Uncle Ben, the woman is crazy. I honestly didn't lead her on."

Once inside the house, they went their separate ways. Nate walked back into the kitchen to find Liberty sitting at the table with Christina and Toni.

"Everything okay?" Toni asked. "When you walked past Grampa's office looking murderous, I figured I'd better have Craig and Uncle Ben follow you."

So that's how they knew I was out there. "Thanks for that." He turned his attention to Liberty and reached for her hand. "Let's go somewhere and talk."

At first, Nate thought about them leaving, but she needed to start hanging around people. Positive people. Nate couldn't think of any better place for her to make some connections and maybe even befriend some of his cousins.

When he saw that his grandfather's office was empty, he escorted her in and closed the door. She hadn't said anything to him, but he wasn't deterred. Still holding her hand, he led her to the sofa and sat next to her.

"I'm not sure what's going on in that beautiful head of yours, but I can explain about Angel."

Nate told her how he and Angel had been over before Liberty came back into his life. He also told her about the calls and his encounter with her at the restaurant.

"Just in case you had any doubt, I'm a one-woman man and would never cheat on you."

Liberty glanced down at their joined hands before returning her attention to him. "I know, but...yeah, I did wonder."

"Baby, I will always be straight with you. I love you." She gasped, her hand covering her mouth. "Only you."

"Oh, Nate. I love you too." She flung her arms around his neck and he held her tightly. "I have always loved you."

Nate cradled the back of her head and kissed her. He wanted her to feel how much he cared about her and wanted her in his life. She moaned, clutching his shoulders when he deepened the kiss. Now he wished they were at his place because the last thing he wanted to do was stop. He hadn't planned to profess his love at that moment, but he meant every word and it was past time he told her.

When he finally let her up for air, he asked, "Are we good regarding Angel?"

Liberty nodded. "Yes."

"Now, about our conversation earlier. Thank you for telling me about the baby. I hate you went through that. I know it couldn't have been easy going through it by yourself."

"Sometimes when I look back on those years, I can't believe that was my life. And though my heart was ripped out when my baby girl died, I—"

"A girl? You knew what you were having?"

Liberty nodded and glanced away. She bit down on her lower lip and inhaled before releasing the breath slowly. Nate said nothing while she pulled herself together.

"My life might've been awful then, but had she been born, both of our lives would've been hell. I can't even imagine how hard it would've been getting away from Isaac with my baby."

Nate didn't even want to think about that. He'd heard of people killing for less. A custody war with a man like Isaac would have destroyed Liberty.

"I saw the way you looked at Chanelle earlier. Can you...can you still have children? Do you want children?"

"According to my doctor at the time, physically I'm fine. Emotionally... Nate, I don't know if I can go through that again. Losing a child, it felt as if someone had reached inside my chest, grabbed hold of my heart and yanked it out. Crushing it beneath their feet. It was...it was... I can't even describe the loss I felt."

Nate hugged her again. Unsure of what to say. He wanted a family more than anything, and he wanted it with her. But if she didn't want to take a chance on having another child, it wasn't a deal breaker.

Liberty lifted her head, her eyelashes laced with tears. "I love children, Nate. And honestly, given the right circumstances... If ever I'm blessed to get pregnant again, I would welcome that child into my life."

He smiled and kissed her lips. That's all he needed to hear. He planned to spend the rest of his life with this woman, and they could cross that bridge when they got to it.

"Okay, let's backtrack to our previous conversation. *Angel.* She's been watching us, and I don't trust her."

Chapter Twenty-One

"I guess now that you're madly and passionately in love, you have forgotten all about your little sister. You haven't called me in days," Demi griped on the other end of the phone.

Liberty laughed, holding the cell phone between her ear and shoulder as she removed a lentil and quinoa salad from the refrigerator and placed it on the counter. She had prepared several dishes for dinner and absolutely loved cooking in Nate's kitchen.

"You should be glad I have a man. Now I don't have to monopolize all of your time or be the third-wheel on your dates. I'm sure Alan was about ready to ship me back to Chicago."

"Don't be silly. He loves you almost as much as I do."

"Yeah, sure he does."

"So, is your honey home yet?"

Liberty smiled at the endearment. She never thought she could be this happy. It had been three weeks since she and Nate expressed their love for one another. To say he was a dream come true would be an understatement.

She glanced at the clock on the microwave. "He should be pulling into the garage any minute now."

"What about his stalker? Has she made an appearance?" Demi asked.

"Nope. As far as I know, he hasn't heard from Angel. She didn't even show up for the protective order hearing, and Nate was able to get the restraining order. She can't come within five hundred feet of either of us."

Liberty had freaked out a little when Nate told her that Angel had been watching them. The idea he had a stalker, who knew he was dating someone else, was uncomfortable and scary. The first couple of weeks, he hadn't wanted her driving or going anywhere alone, which was fine with Liberty. A woman scorned was nothing to play around with. But this week, she insisted on driving herself to and from work since she had a new project that required site visits.

"I'm glad Nate's taking this situation serious, especially since this woman has seen you with him. Did you take him up on his offer to move in with him?"

"Nope, I still have my place."

"Sis, what are you waiting for? You're there most of the time anyway, and his house is much safer than your apartment."

Liberty loved Nate's home and felt comfortable in it, but they weren't married. Until or if that happened, she planned to keep her apartment, and that's what she explained to her sister. Besides, she loved her new independence. Gone were the days of just speaking positive affirmations about being a strong, confident, successful woman. She was finally feeling like that woman. Yes, she would marry Nate in a heartbeat, but in the meantime, she would continue building her life and pursuing her goals.

"Alright, Demi. I need to get off this phone so I can finish up dinner before my *honey* gets home." They said their goodbyes just as Liberty heard the garage door opening.

*

Nate pulled into his driveway glad to see Liberty's car. He had given her a house key a couple of weeks ago, but today was the first time she had actually used it.

Why didn't she park in the garage? Normally, he parked his SUV and BMW in there, but whenever she stayed over, he pulled the SUV out and left it in the driveway.

He went ahead and parked inside. He'd move the cars around after dinner.

"Hey, baby. Something smells good," Nate called out when he walked into the house, leaving his briefcase near the garage door. He strolled into the kitchen and found Liberty bent over checking on something in the oven. He had the perfect view of her fine ass encased in the short skirt. Actually, the whole ensemble, including the fitted red sweater and her bare feet, had his shaft twitching. Everything about the woman turned him on.

"Hey there," she said smiling up at him and setting a pan of something that smelled amazing on the stove top.

"I love coming home to you and a home cooked meal." He palmed her butt, giving it a gentle squeeze as he nibbled on her neck. No doubt she felt his excitement pressed against her back.

"I love being here."

She turned in his arms and lifted up on tip-toe to place a kiss on his lips. When she went to pull away, he maintained his hold and gave her a long, heated kiss.

"Mmm, and I love when you greet me like this," she mumbled when the kiss ended.

"You could get that every night if you moved in with me." Not only did Nate love having her in his space, but he also wanted her out of that apartment. The neighborhood wasn't safe enough as far as he was concerned.

She pushed against his chest and went back to the stove. "How was your day?"

He let her change the subject, not as irritated as usual that she kept shooting down the idea. Her excuse was that she needed to put all of her focus on passing the bar. Though he agreed, and wanted to do anything to help her pass, he hoped that was all that was keeping her from accepting his offer.

"Can you grab the glasses and the bottle of sparkling grape juice on the counter near the refrigerator?" she asked and headed to the dining room.

"Wow, it looks great in here." Nate stood at the entrance and took in the fancy place settings and the tall, tapered candles illuminating the space. Normally, when at his place, they had their meals at the breakfast bar or in front of the television. This was a nice change. "What's the occasion?"

"I just wanted to do something nice for you."

"You always do nice things for me." She went out of her way with thoughtful deeds, like having lunch delivered to him at work occasionally. Or whenever he stopped by her apartment after work, she would have a cold beer waiting for him. Those small gestures meant a lot to him.

"I hope you like the veggie enchilada casserole. It's a new recipe."

He pulled her to his side and kissed the top of her head. "I love everything you cook, but you know I pretty much eat anything."

"Well, if you ever get tired of having vegetarian dishes, tell me."

He agreed even though he probably wouldn't ever tell her.

They sat at the table, eating and talking like an old married couple. The conversation ranged in topics from politics to a new app he wanted her to check out. The more time they spent together, the more time Nate wanted to spend with her. There were times he forgot that they'd been apart for so many years considering how well they got along. He was ready to make her a permanent fixture in his life and his home but wanted to make sure she was ready.

When they were done eating, Nate asked, "Did you study already?"

"As a matter of fact, I did. I had a short day and went to the library after work. So tonight I'm all yours."

She wiggled her eyebrows and Nate grinned. He could think of a number of things he'd like to do with her, or to her, but refrained from suggesting his first idea. Considering he usually ravished her whenever she was in his home, he didn't want her to think he had a one-track mind.

"How about we pop some popcorn, curl up in front of the TV, and watch a movie?" he suggested.

Liberty stood, lifted her sweater over her head, and dramatically tossed it over her shoulder. Arousal crawled through Nate's body and a smile spread slowly across his mouth.

To hell with a movie. If she wanted to strip for him instead, who was he to deprive her of that pleasure?

Liberty moved slowly, taking the long way around the table and doing a good job at making his body yearn for her. During the last few months, Nate had watched this sweetheart of a woman come into her own. Those traces of defeat that had caused her to doubt herself, as well as her abilities, were gone. In their place was a determined, independent woman who had suffered through life's hard knocks, but survived, coming out stronger because of them.

His woman.

She was all his.

Moving toward him, the gentle sway of her hips kept him transfixed as his pulse inched up.

She hiked up her skirt giving him just enough of a peek at her lace panties to make his shaft leap to attention. He had a feeling that was intentional as she straddled him. And while he enjoyed this little seduction performance, Nate was so ready to get her naked.

He placed his hand on her bare thighs, knowing if he touched any other part of her, he was going to lose it.

"I actually had something else in mind for tonight," she mumbled against his mouth, nibbling on his top lip and then his lower one. She undid his tie, letting it glide to the floor, and then went to work on the buttons of his shirt.

Blood shot from Nate's brain straight to his groin within a heartbeat when she started grinding against him.

He groaned, his pulse amped up. He tightened his grip on her thighs struggling to maintain his control. "This is way better than the movie that I had in mind," he said, getting harder with every swirl of her hip. No way could he sit there and let her torture him with this little game she had going.

Liberty fumbled with the buttons on his dress shirt, moaning and squirming as Nate kissed, then sucked on her neck. Grinding her hips against the bulge in his pants was supposed to get a rise out of him. But now that his large hands had moved from her thighs, slipped under the skirt and grabbed hold of her butt, her control was shot.

Nate's fingers kneaded her bottom, pulling her tighter against his groin. So much for trying to seduce him. He damn near had her panting.

Moaning, Liberty pulled back and unsnapped the front of her bra, tossing it to the floor. His mouth continued its delicious assault on her heated skin, but then she placed her hands on the side of his face. The move immediately stopped the sweet torture as she zoned in on the fierce hunger in his eyes.

"I want you...now," she said.

"Good, because I'm about to explode."

She squeaked and threw her arms around his neck when he stood suddenly, carrying her quickly out of the room. She almost laughed at his eagerness, loving how easy it was to get him all hot and bothered. When he didn't head for the stairs that led to the bedroom, she started to protest, but he cut her off.

"No time for stairs. I need to be inside you now."

"What about the candles?"

"I'll take care of them later." He practically dropped her on the leather sofa in the family room and shook roughly out of his shirt, only to get hung up on the cufflinks.

"Dammit!" he growled.

Liberty giggled while he fumbled with his attire. She hurried and unfastened her skirt, pushing it and her panties down her legs before kicking the garments off.

"You make me crazy," Nate said on a husky groan, still clothed from the waist down when he covered her naked body. "And you smell so damn good."

There he went, torturing her again with sizzling kisses against her neck. His hand slid down the side of her body and stopped at one of her breasts. Tweaking, his fingers taunted her taut nipple before he teased it with the pad of his thumb. He moved lower down her body, and his mouth soon replaced his fingers. Pushing her breasts together, he kneaded them as he sucked and then swirled his tongue around each nipple.

A ferocious flare of yearning seized Liberty.

"Okay, okay, I give. I'm ready," she gasped for air, practically whining while her hands scrambled around for Nate's belt buckle. She didn't need foreplay. All she wanted was to feel him buried deep inside of her. If only she could undo his pants. "*Nate.*"

"I know, baby."

Nate sat up, dug out his wallet and a condom while she undid his belt and zipper. He sucked in a breath when she cupped him. Enjoying the power she had over him, her hand glided up and down his length with an intermittent squeeze.

"Babe," he growled, drawing out the word.

Not bothering to remove his pants completely, he quickly sheathed himself. Before she could take her next breath, he was buried inside of her.

Liberty gasped and arched her back as he slid in and out of her slick entrance like a man possessed.

Harder. Faster. Nate pumped, going deeper each time he pushed into her. She thrust her hips upward. A surge of pleasure roared through her body as they rocked in perfect harmony, their moves growing jerky with each stroke.

Liberty moaned. Her hold on Nate's shoulders tighten as an orgasm mounted within her, and like a strike of a match, a flame ignited, and she climaxed. Everything in her exploded in a downpour of fiery sensations.

Seconds later, Nate's release hit him hard. "Liberty!" he growled as his body stiffened before he collapsed on top of her.

They lay panting, Nate's face in the crook of her neck, his hot breath heating her skin. Sex with him was quickly becoming her favorite activity, but the quickies were downright addictive.

"Yep, this idea was definitely better than any damn movie," he said still breathing hard. "Now, let's finish this upstairs."

Chapter Twenty-Two

"Nate, I'm getting ready to leave!" Liberty yelled up the stairs. He'd been in the shower when she left the master bedroom twenty minutes ago. She wasn't sure if he could hear her, but she was too lazy to walk all the way back up the stairs.

Liberty glanced at her cell phone, noting she had forty-five minutes to get to work. Hopefully, there wouldn't be much traffic.

"Nate!"

"I can stop by the site on my way to work. Are you going to be there?" Nate said into the cell phone plastered to his ear. He buttoned his beige dress shirt as he lumbered down the stairs. "Okay, well hold on a second. Better yet, let me call you right back after I walk Liberty out."

"I'm sorry, honey. I didn't realize you were on the phone," she said when he ended the call, but giggled when he wrapped her in a bear hug, littering her face with feathery kisses.

God, she loved this man.

"I'm glad you didn't leave without saying bye." He planted a real kiss on her lips and a shiver ran through her body. This man...this sweet, sexy, attentive man delivered the most intoxicating kisses Liberty had ever experienced. She never imagined that a romantic relationship would be in her future, but each day with Nate was like a fantasy come true.

He lifted his head slightly and cupped her face between his large hands to stare into her eyes. "Do you have any idea how much I love you?"

Liberty grinned at hearing her three favorite words. "Um, maybe a little, but I love you more." They played kissy-face for a bit longer before he released her. "Am I going to see you tonight?" she asked while slipping into her coat. The temperature had dropped significantly over the last couple of weeks. She grabbed her bag as they strolled to the door.

"Yeah, but it'll be pretty late. Me and Uncle Ben have a meeting tonight near the airport. I'll call you before I come by."

They walked outside. "You don't have to call. I'll be up studying. So come by whenever... Oh my God! My car!" she shrieked and raced toward the vehicle, but Nate stopped her by wrapping his arm around her waist.

He cursed under his breath. Her car looked as if it had been caught in a war zone. Every window was bashed in and the tires slashed.

A wave of fear swept through her body and she glanced around frantically. She saw no one, but her anxiety amped up.

"Let's get back inside." Nate pushed her behind him as he backed them to the front door. The moment they were safely inside, he locked the door and called 911.

Like a zombie waking after a hundred years, Liberty lowered her bag to the floor, shocked by what she'd just seen. She ran her hands up and down her arms, trying to stop trembling as she paced back and forth. Had Angel done this? If so, why now? They hadn't heard anything from her in weeks. At least as far as Liberty knew.

"I don't give a damn what has to be done!" Nate yelled into the phone. "I want her ass arrested!"

Liberty rubbed her neck, scared that this woman was after her now. Her car was old and probably ready for the junkyard, but it still got her from point A to point B. She couldn't afford new windows and tires, and she definitely couldn't afford a new car.

That last thought brought a whole new round of fear. What if the woman had done something else to the car? For all Liberty knew, there could be a bomb attached to it.

She looked up when Nate ended his call.

"What type of sick person does something like this?" she spat. The fear she'd felt moments ago had quickly turned to anger. "The car might not look like much, but it's all I have."

Nate released a frustrated breath. "I'll buy you another car."

"That's not the point, Nate!"

"Baby, I know you're upset." He moved toward her. Liberty wasn't sure what he saw on her face, but he stopped abruptly.

"Upset?" she said through gritted teeth. "I'm not upset. I'm mad as hell! I have worked my ass off for everything I have! Now some lunatic comes along and destroys my means of transportation. All because I have someone she wants! Who does that? What type of satisfaction comes from doing that to me? Does she think you'll want her now?"

Liberty turned her back on Nate and wanted to scream or pound on something. She whipped back around.

"Every *damn* time I take a few steps forward, shit like this happens! And I'm sick of it!" she screamed. She swiped her arm across the top of a nearby shelf, sending a vase and picture frames flying across the room. Glass littered the floor as her body trembled with pent up frustration. "I can't handle any more. I'm tired of one thing after another ruining my progress."

Nate said nothing. He didn't move, and she could barely tell if he was breathing. But the love shining in his eyes was unmistakable.

"Are you done?" he finally asked.

Liberty's shoulders sagged like a balloon that had just been popped with a needle. "Yes."

Without another word, Nate pulled her roughly against his body and held her tightly. Being in his arms always brought a peace that transcended all understanding. She felt safe, protected, and most importantly, she felt loved.

"When you took those steps forward, that you mentioned a few minutes ago, you took them alone. The difference now—you have me. So when shit like this happens, I'll be right there with you. I'm not going anywhere."

*

Later that night, Nate stood in the doorway of his bedroom. He brought his beer bottle to his lips and took a swig as he stared at Liberty's sleeping form.

Considering the day had started with some good lovemaking, it had soon gone downhill. All day he had tried to make sense of Angel's actions. According to the detectives that had been assigned to the case, maliciously destroying someone's vehicle was considered a felony. They had spent over an hour questioning him and Liberty about Angel and asking if they had any other enemies. But tonight, they called to inform…

"Nooo."

Nate's gaze snapped to the bed. Liberty's head thrashed back and forth against the pillow as she mumbled in her sleep.

Nate hurried across the room and set his beer on the nightstand. The moment he sat on the bed next to Liberty, she bolted upright. Breathing hard with perspiration lacing her hairline, she placed her hand on her chest trying to catch her breath.

"Hey," Nate said, rubbing her back to let her know he was there and to offer some comfort. Once she settled down, he pulled her against him and leaned against the headboard. "Bad dream?"

"Yeah."

"Want to talk about it?"

Liberty shook her head. "No. What time is it?"

"Almost nine o'clock."

She had been asleep for the last two hours. Once the detectives left that morning, Liberty had insisted on going to work. She claimed that taking the day off would give Angel power over her. Nate didn't agree but had lost the battle of getting her to stay home with him. He had taken her to work and then went into the office. He hadn't stayed long since he couldn't concentrate.

"Have you heard anything from the detectives?" Liberty asked, interrupting Nate's thoughts.

When he hesitated, she leaned back and looked up at him.

"I just got off the phone with one of them."

Now fully awake, Liberty straightened. "Did they find her?"

"Yes."

"Oh thank, God. I didn't think they'd find her that fast."

"She didn't do it."

Liberty froze. "What? What do you mean she didn't do it?"

"Angel has been in Atlanta for the past two weeks. Seems she put in for a transfer with her company and relocated. The detectives spoke with her and her supervisor. She has a solid alibi."

"Then who did this? Who would destroy my car?"

"They're still investigating but…"

"But what?"

"But they're going to look into Isaac."

Liberty remained quiet before saying, "He wouldn't do this."

Nate frowned. "What do you mean he wouldn't do this? Why not? He could still be angry about the divorce. Hell, he's done worse."

Liberty shook her head and moved to the side of the bed, lowering her feet to the floor. "Isaac is all about playing mental games with people. He wouldn't stoop to damaging someone's vehicle. And with my car, he'd assume it was of no value to me, and wouldn't bother. No, if Isaac wanted to get to me, or get inside my head, it wouldn't be like this. He would go after something that meant the world to me," she paused and raised her gaze to Nate. "Or he would go after someone I love."

They stared at each other for a minute before Nate said, "Does he know you're in Cincinnati?"

Liberty shrugged. "I don't know. Since the divorce, I haven't heard from him. Though, I didn't tell him I was relocating, he has the means to get any information he wants. Even with my name change, if he wanted to find me, he would. I don't think it's him."

Nate sighed, closed his eyes, and pinched the bridge of his nose. How the hell could he protect either of them from an unknown enemy?

Liberty curled up against him. "What are we going to do?"

"I don't know, babe, but we're going to get to the bottom of this."

Chapter Twenty-Three

"You look absolutely stunning tonight. I'm the envy of every man in the room," Nate whispered close to Liberty's ear, his arm possessively around her waist. She was wearing a short, navy blue cocktail dress that Demi and Christina had helped her find during a shopping trip earlier that day. The wide neckline and fitted bodice vintage outfit was different from what she would have normally chosen.

Liberty smiled up at Nate. "Thank you."

They were attending a networking banquet hosted by Cincinnati's local business owners club. Weeks ago, Nate had asked her to be his date, and at first Liberty had been hesitant. After being ostracized by Isaac and key players in Chicago's business world, she wasn't sure she was ready to put herself out there again. But lately, with Nate by her side, she felt invincible.

Despite the past week of looking over her shoulder and being chauffeured around by him or other men in his family, Liberty's life was perfect. Daily she had to pinch herself to ensure she wasn't dreaming. Her and Nate's reunion had blossomed into a relationship that had exceeded her expectations, and Liberty believed in love again. After the divorce, she'd been in survival mode. Trying to do all she could to prove that she wasn't a failure. Fate had indeed surprised her.

"Excuse me, ol' protective one."

Liberty and Nate turned to find Christina standing with her arms folded across her chest and a smirk on her face. Tonight, she had her long curly hair pinned on top of her head in an intricate style. Her pretty face was makeup free except for lipstick and she too was dressed in a vintage dress. The black A-line, lace dress was cinched at the waist and flowed into a full, tulle skirt that stopped mid-calf.

"Are you going to let Liberty out of your sight at all tonight?"

"I hadn't planned on it," Nate said seriously, and Liberty shook her head. "Where's your husband? Shouldn't you be bothering Luke instead of trying to steal my date away?"

Luke, a defense attorney who had grown up in New York but relocated to Cincinnati to be with Christina, was like no lawyer Liberty had ever met. Martina referred to him as the family's thug lawyer. He was a nice enough guy, and crazy intelligent, but there was definitely a lethal edge to him.

"He's on his way. He told me to hang out with you guys until he arrived," she said to Nate. "Now, getting back to you. Liberty's too sweet to say this, but you're smothering her."

"Whoa, wait," Liberty chimed in. "Yes, he might be a little overprotective, but smothering is too harsh of a term. With that said though, I do think he can loosen up some. Right, honey?" She batted her eyes at Nate, knowing the gesture would get a rise out of him. Sure enough, the left corner of his lip inched up into a slight smile.

"Good, it's settled. Lib, I wanna introduce you to the woman I was telling you about earlier. The one who owns a chain of vegetarian restaurants throughout the Midwest."

"Oh, wow. I didn't know she would be here. Definitely introduce me." Liberty started to move away from Nate, but he held tight and she sighed. "Really, Nate? I'm not leaving the building. I'll meet the lady and then come and find you. Okay?"

"*God*, you are such a worrywart," Christina said to her cousin and looped her arm through Liberty's. "Let's go."

Liberty glanced back at Nate who was still staring after her, his face stoic. It wasn't until she smiled and blew him a kiss that he seemed to relax.

*

Nate grabbed a drink from the bar outside of the banquet room. He thought about going in search of his uncle who was also attending the event. Instead, he roamed around the atrium, stopped and chatted with a few people before moving on.

Still a little concerned about Liberty's safety, he glanced around in search of her and Christina. He spotted them near the bar at the other end of the hall, each holding a glass. He wasn't worried about Liberty drinking. True to her word, she hadn't had alcohol since that night at the bar.

Nate released a contented sigh. Who would've known that rescuing her from a stranger at the bar months ago, would catapult her back into his life?

He sipped his scotch and watched as she spoke to a woman standing next to Christina, and a bout of pride gripped him. He was so damn proud of his woman. Strong and determined, Liberty had truly reclaimed her life. She was thriving at work, juggling several projects, and in less than a month, she would take the bar. In his eyes, she was a modern day Super Woman.

Nate took one last look in their direction before heading into the banquet room to go in search of his uncle. He spotted Ben speaking with two other men, and as if sensing his presence, Ben glanced in Nate's direction.

"I didn't mean for you to stop what you were doing," Nate said when Ben approached him.

"No problem. I'd been trying to get away from those two for the last thirty minutes. You know how attorneys are when they get together. All they do is talk shop."

Nate laughed. "You do remember that you're a lawyer, right? And you probably yap as much as they do."

Ben took a sip of the dark liquid in his glass. "Don't be a wise ass. I'm not as bad as they are."

"Uh, yeah, right." Nate chuckled again and glanced around at the small groups of people spread about the large room. "The last time I attended this event, there hadn't been this many people here."

"You're right. Each year the event gets bigger and better. Probably because they've been able to attract more prominent keynote speakers."

Ben gave a nod of greeting to a senator whose name Nate didn't know. His uncle seemed to know everyone in the city. They had yet to go anyplace together where Ben wasn't recognized.

"Well, it looks like the Jenkins family is well represented tonight."

Nate and Ben turned at the sound of the gravelly voice to find one of their grandfather's golfing buddies.

"Benjamin Jenkins. How the heck are you, son?"

"I'm well. How's it going, Mr. Evans?" Ben shook the older gentleman's hand. "Do you remember my nephew, Nathaniel?"

Evans squinted instead of using the glasses that were tucked into the breast pocket of his suit jacket. "Aren't you one of Sarah and Lewis's boys?"

"Yes, sir." Nate shook his hand.

"How is everyone? I haven't been to one of the Sunday brunches in a while. That's how I used to keep up with all of you."

"Everyone is doing well."

While the two caught up, Nate tuned out, thinking about the conversation he'd had with the detective that was on the case. The Jenkins family was fine, but whoever had vandalized Liberty's car was still at large. Nate found it hard to believe that no one saw or heard anything that night, not even him and Liberty. So far, there hadn't been anymore incidents, but the nagging feeling of dread crept into Nate's body periodically. He wanted whoever had done this found.

He tuned back into the conversation between Ben and Evans in time to catch the old man discussing the event's keynote speaker, Aubrey Mahan. Nate looked forward to hearing Aubrey speak again. He had first met the multi-millionaire a few years ago at a business symposium in New York. Impressed with his presentation on how he made his first million, Nate had sought him out at the end of that event. Turned out that Aubrey was a down-to-earth guy and whenever Nate was in New York, they hooked up for drinks.

"It's too bad he couldn't make it tonight. He—"

"What? I hadn't heard," Nate cut in. "Aubrey's not here."

The old man shook his head. "I heard earlier that he had a family emergency and had to cancel, but the organizers were able to find another speaker."

"Who did they end up getting?" Ben asked, draining his glass.

"A guy out of Chicago. Have you heard of the Culpeppers?"

Unease radiated through Nate, and Ben cast him a steely glance, probably thinking the same thing.

"One of the kids, a big-time lawyer," Evans continued, not noticing Nate and Ben's discomfort. "I think the name is Ian...no, wait. Maybe it was Isaac. Isaac Culpepper."

Chapter Twenty-Four

"I'll be back," Christina told Liberty. "I need to call Luke to see what's keeping him. He should've been here by now. Where are you going to be?"

"Actually, I'm going to the lady's room. Then I'll probably go and find Nate. I think I saw him walk into the banquet room. We'll meet you in there."

"Sounds good," Christina said before hurrying away.

"Hello, Kayla."

Liberty startled at the deep voice she thought she would never hear again. She whirled around, causing her club soda to slosh over the rim of the glass.

"Isaac," she said flatly, holding her arm away from her body, hoping she hadn't gotten any pop on her dress.

Wiping her wrist with the small napkin she'd had around the glass, Liberty realized the hatred she'd harbored for this man for years had subsided. She no longer had the desire to claw his eyes out or throat punch him for treating her like trash.

"What are you doing here?"

"I could ask you the same thing. Do you live in Cincinnati now?"

She studied his eyes and knew immediately he was asking a question he already knew the answer to. Another uncomfortable thought filtered into her mind. Had he been the one to destroy her car?

Liberty shook the thought free. Vandalizing vehicles was child's play to someone like Isaac.

"What are you doing here?" Liberty asked again.

"Would you believe that I missed you? That I'm here to beg for your forgiveness in hopes you'll come back to me?"

"No. Try again."

He chuckled, the sound as irritating as his presence. "I'm the keynote speaker this evening."

Oh, that's just great.

Liberty tried schooling her expression, but wasn't sure if she pulled it off considering the smirk on his face.

"Good for you." He might've been a jerk, but he was a masterful business man. If those in attendance could learn how to make even half as much money as he'd made, more power to them. She didn't know if she could handle sitting through dinner with him speaking to the group, but no way would she give him the satisfaction of leaving. She'd have to stick it out.

Oh crap. Nate was going to blow a gasket for more reasons than one. He'd been looking forward to hearing Aubrey somebody speak. Now, not only would he find out Isaac was there, but that he was also the guest speaker.

"I never thought you would leave Chicago. I know how much you loved the city," Isaac said. "I guess living on the streets gets old after a while, huh?"

"And I guess being an asshole is still how you roll, huh?"

He threw his head back and laughed as if she had told the funniest joke. Anyone looking at them from a distance would think they were old friends catching up. They would never guess how far from the truth that was. This man, dressed in an expensive suit that was tailored to fit his slim body and make him look every bit the wealthy man he was, was actually the devil in disguise.

"That was one thing I always liked about you, Kayla. Your quick wit and sassy mouth." His gaze settled on her lips and made her skin crawl. No one could argue that he wasn't a nice-looking man, but everything about him made her want to puke.

Recalling the times she'd lay there and let him kiss her while her mind was on Nate made her disgusted with herself. Though she couldn't stand Isaac, she hated herself for making that ridiculous deal with him. Foregoing her happiness to take care of her family was a sacrifice she had to make. But had she been stronger and smarter, she would have thought out the situation better. She could have delayed law school and found a job somewhere to help cover her mother's medical expenses, as well as help get them back on their feet. Instead, she sold her soul to the devil and went through life ashamed of her decision.

"Funny, I received a call from some detectives on your behalf earlier this week," Isaac interrupted her thoughts. "I can't believe you would think I'd waste my time ripping apart a damn car. Don't you know me better than that?"

"I know you better than I care to admit, and all that I know, I'm trying to forget."

He flashed that wicked grin that reminded her of The Joker from the batman movies. "Same old Kayla."

Liberty hated that name, especially when it came from his mouth.

"I have to admit, though. You're looking good. I guess life is treating you well…for now. I'm sure with your luck it won't last."

"Is that a threat, Isaac? Are you back to undermining everything I set out to do for your own pleasure?" Anger bubbled inside her. For years, especially after she lost their baby, she allowed him to talk down to her. After a while she started to believe the nonsense he spewed. Now was different. She was different. Funny how when you're surrounded by people who love you, everything looked and felt brighter.

He moved in closer, but Liberty stood her ground. "I never threaten."

Liberty nodded. "You're right. You don't. I know firsthand how evil you are and what you're capable of, but I survived. So whatever else you have planned for me, bring it. I'm not afraid and I sure as hell am not running from you."

There was that grin again. The darkness of it sent chills through Liberty's body. She braced herself for whatever he planned to say. He might have held her down in the past with nasty words, but she refused to give him that same power ever again.

"Someone as beautiful as you shouldn't keep company with bastards who tend to suck the life out everything in their reach," Nate said in an intense, low voice as if straining to stay in control. Liberty hadn't heard his approach, but was glad he was there. His arm slid around her waist, and his gaze nailed Isaac in place.

The arrogant smirk that had been covering her ex-husband's mouth since invading her space moments earlier fell. Liberty didn't miss the way his breathing changed and how his jaw clenched hard enough to shatter his teeth.

"Well, Kayla, I see you found your way back to your college crush. You couldn't handle a real man so you're settling for a punk-ass boy-toy. Figures."

Nate dropped his arm from around her and made a move toward Isaac. Liberty stopped him by fisting the back of his jacket within her hands. There was no way she was letting him stoop to Isaac's level. Her ex-husband thrived on getting a reaction out of people. He wouldn't let Nate get away with hitting him again the way he had years ago. No, Isaac would do everything in his power to ruin Nate.

Seeing people looking in their direction, Liberty spoke in a low voice to Nate. "Not here. Besides, he's not worth the trouble. Let's go in and find our seats."

With herculean strength, she pulled Nate in the opposite direction.

"We're not staying," he ground out and redirected them toward the closest exit holding her hand tight enough to crush it.

"Nate, we're staying," she hissed, and put on the brakes. He looked at her as if she'd lost her mind.

"What do you mean we're staying? There's no way in hell I can sit through a minute of anything his pompous ass has to say."

"I know, honey, but I can't leave. I can't give him the satisfaction of knowing that he rocked me by showing up here tonight. I can't let him win."

Nate saw the pleading in her eyes, but that didn't slow his heart from practically beating out of his chest. There was nothing he wouldn't do for her, but this... He didn't know if he could share the same room with the bastard knowing all that he had done to her.

Nate had almost lost his shit when he spotted them across the hall in a heated discussion. Only his uncle warning him to be cool, and the number of influential people in attendance, kept him from acting a fool. Nick was usually the one who threw a punch first and then asked questions, but tonight Nate came close to doing the same thing.

"Please, honey. I need to do this."

Nate cursed under his breath and cupped her face between his hands. "You know I can't handle it when you look at me like that with those exotic eyes. Alright, we'll stay." He kissed her red lips.

He hoped he wasn't making a mistake in agreeing to stick around. He understood her need to flex her independence, but in this case, he didn't like it.

"If at any time you want to get out of here, just say the word."

Her sexy lips tipped up into that sweet smile that always made his heart flip inside his chest.

"I will, and thank you. I know it's not going to be easy, for either of us, but I appreciate you being here for me."

"Always, baby. I will *always* be here for you."

Chapter Twenty-Five

Liberty walked into LCA tired from a long night of studying, but feeling more encouraged than she'd felt in a long time. Her life was on track. She didn't love her job, but it was paying the bills, and she had proven to herself that she was marketable. Her plans were to take the bar, and pass it. Then she would look for another job. Until then, she'd buy her time at LCA.

"What's up, Liberty?" John, a guy from the maintenance crew greeted. He had never come on to her outright, but each time he looked at her it felt as if he was picturing her naked.

"Hi, John," she said and kept walking.

John's creepiness made her think about the run-in with Isaac the week before. Liberty thought the last time she saw him in Chicago would be the last time, but no such luck. It felt good standing up to him.

Liberty took the stairs up to the second floor, and when she stepped into her office, she was greeted by the fresh scent of flowers. A smile covered her face. Nate had sent the gorgeous bouquet the day before.

She leaned over them and inhaled. "God, these smell good."

The arrangement, a gorgeous mixture of white Asiatic lilies, white roses, and white mini carnations, brightened the whole space. Nate had been the only man to ever send her flowers. Once he learned that, he started having them delivered weekly. His thoughtful gestures, everything from letting her use his SUV, to preparing relaxing bubble baths, had her falling deeper and deeper in love with him. It felt so good to have a supportive man in her corner.

She dropped down in her chair and lifted the note that someone had left on her desk.

See me in my office when you get in. Eden

Excitement buzzed inside of Liberty. The award announcement for Unity Tower was expected any day. Maybe Eden had heard something. If awarded, this would be Liberty's second successful proposal. Being with the company for almost six months, she had submitted two bids for the company, as well as two state proposals. The Unity Tower project had been the largest. In addition to that, she was overseeing two additional jobs that were on target to finish ahead of schedule.

Feeling encouraged, she quickly stored her purse in the bottom draw of the desk and headed to the third floor.

"Hey Liberty," Eden's assistant greeted. "You can go on in."

"Thanks." She knocked before entering. "Morning, Eden. You wanted to see me?"

"Yes, come in. Have a seat." She pointed to one of the chairs in front of her desk. "Give me a second to finish this email."

Eden went back to typing something into her computer. Liberty swept her gaze over the woman. Tall with shocking red hair and pale skin, Eden had been with the company for over thirty years. Working her way up from an administrative assistant position, she knew practically everything about the company and the procedures. She might've respected Eden's success, but there wasn't much love between them.

The woman didn't like Liberty. There were never any congratulations on a job well done. There were also times when Eden gave projects, but didn't give enough information to complete the job successfully. It was good Liberty asked a lot of questions.

"I was informed this morning," Eden said interrupting Liberty's thoughts, "that LCA won the bid for the Unity Tower project." Her words were spoken very business-like with all the enthusiasm of a saltine cracker. Liberty looked past her boss's sourness and did a happy dance inside. She was two-for-two in awarded proposals for the company, and she could barely contain her excitement.

"That's great news! Do we have to change anything or was the proposal accepted as is?"

"LCA should receive details in the mail by the end of the week. But something else has been brought to my attention." Eden finally looked at Liberty. "I hear that you're *involved* with one of our business partners."

Surprised and a bit confused, Liberty tilted her head. "What business partner?"

"Nathaniel Jenkins."

"Technically he's not a business partner. The company he works for is possibly collaborating with LCA, but the final documents haven't been signed," Liberty said, knowing it was only a matter of time before LCA received the award letter and contract.

Eden studied her, probably wondering if Liberty was trying to imply that Jenkins & Sons might not do business with them.

"Whatever he is, LCA frowns on its employees sleeping with clients, partners, or anyone who can cause problems for the company."

Alarm bells erupted within Liberty as she gathered her thoughts, wanting to be careful with her response. She was friendly with her co-workers, but not close enough to any of them to share details about her and Nate's relationship. Then she thought about something Nate had said. *Everyone in town knows someone in the Jenkins family.*

"What's this really about, Eden? LCA doesn't have a no-fraternizing policy regarding employees dating each other.

Nor is there anything written that states I can't have a relationship with anyone remotely affiliated with LCA."

"That might be so, but it's still not a good look. Either you stop seeing Mr. Jenkins, or we're going to have to terminate your employment immediately."

"You can't do that!" Liberty snapped.

"I can. You're still on probation. We can let you go for any reason."

Liberty released a humorless laugh wanting to snatch the woman up by her hair and shake her. "Unbelievable. I have one week left on my probation, and you're trying to pull this nonsense now?"

Anger seized Liberty. It took all she had not to slam her fist against the desk and threaten to sue. Unfortunately, Eden was right. They could let her go for any reason at this point.

"What's it going to be?" The woman glanced at her watch looking bored as she tapped her pen against the desk impatiently. "Mr. Jenkins or your job?"

An angry retort dangled on Liberty's tongue, but her mouth remained shut. She had left Nate once. There was nothing or no one who could make her leave him again.

Liberty stood. "I guess you should get my termination papers together."

"Fine." She grabbed a file folder from one of the drawers in her desk. Pulling out a form, Liberty noticed it had already been filled out.

This is bullshit.

Then something dawned on her. "Who told you that I was involved with Mr. Jenkins?"

"Ted," she said of her supervisor. "He said Lyndon Crawford, LCA's owner, contacted him saying it wasn't good business that you were sleeping with a business partner."

"The owner?" Liberty asked, still trying to process the information. "What makes Crawford think I'm sleeping with Mr. Jenkins?"

"Listen, Liberty. I don't know the details. I told you all that I know and frankly I thought you were smarter. With your skills and education, you could've gone far in this company. Instead, you're throwing this opportunity away for some guy. Do you know how hard it is to find a job?"

If Liberty wasn't so pissed, she might've laughed. She knew better than anyone how hard it was to find a job at her level. But she also knew that what she and Nate had was a second chance at an amazing life together.

LCA's decision to suddenly get rid of her was starting to make sense. Isaac's reach was long and wide. Liberty had found that out the hard way. Had he somehow gotten to the owner of LCA? It was too much of a coincidence for her relationship with Nate to come to the company's attention, especially now. Unfortunately, there wasn't much Liberty could do since she was on probation.

After exit forms were signed, Liberty couldn't get to her office fast enough. When she woke up that morning, this was not how she saw her day going. Losing this job was another setback, but if Isaac was behind her termination, so be it. She wouldn't let him control her life. For the first time since divorcing him, this obstacle didn't feel like the end of the world. She wasn't afraid of the unknown. Another job would come along. In the meantime, she'd spend her days studying, and in February she would take the bar.

"Are you ready to leave, Ms. Stewart?"

She glanced over her shoulder at the doorway to find a security guard.

Unbelievable. I'm being escorted out.

"Yes," she answered.

Liberty grabbed her purse and flowers. With her shoulders back and her head held high, she left the office with the security guard following close behind.

This will all work out.

Chapter Twenty-Six

Nate parked his BMW in front of Liberty's apartment complex and cut the engine. With the light snow covering the roads, soon it would be time to put up his car. But first they needed to get Liberty a new vehicle so he could get his SUV from her.

Nate's gaze took in her block. It wasn't necessarily a bad neighborhood, but he didn't think it was safe enough for a single woman. Since his home was larger, they spent most of their time there. Getting her to stay the night at his place more often was getting easier, but he could tell she treasured her independence. Maybe it was selfish of him to like going home and finding her there, but it was true. Not only was she perfect for him, she fit perfectly in his space. In addition to a key, he had given her a drawer and space in the closet, which she finally started using. Since making their relationship official, he'd seen her every day.

Except today.

Nate climbed out of the car, grabbing the dinner he had prepared, and the bottle of non-alcoholic wine he had picked up on the way. Liberty had called him earlier at work to cancel their plans. That was a first. Something was wrong. She claimed she was fine and planned to relax for the evening. Nate wasn't buying it. He heard the weariness in her voice, and it concerned him. Besides, he'd had big plans for her tonight, and he wasn't about to let her ruin them.

He buzzed her apartment, no longer second-guessing his decision to show up unannounced. He had let her walk away from him once without asking enough questions, but that would never happen again. He couldn't lose her a second time.

"Who's there?"

"Hey, baby, it's me."

She buzzed him in. The hallway was empty, but the smell of fried chicken permeated the air. Nate could hear sounds of a television coming from one of the apartments, and music from another. When he reached Liberty's unit, she was at the door waiting for him.

It didn't matter when, where, or the time of day, the sight of her always revved up his pulse. Seeing her now, he was met with an overwhelming feeling of rightness. She was the woman for him. The woman he wanted to spend the rest of his life with.

"Hi," she said shyly, her smile not quite reaching her beautiful brown eyes.

"Hi, yourself." Nate studied her carefully as she opened the door wider to let him in. "There was no way I could go a day without seeing you."

He set the bags down and shook out of his wool coat, draping it on the back of one of the dining room chairs. He extended his hand to her and she came to him willingly. He held her tight, kissing the side of her head as he inhaled her familiar scent of lavender.

Not able to wait another minute to taste her, he lowered his mouth and covered hers. Sweetness. Her lips were soft and inviting. What started as a gentle greeting quickly turned into something more heated. He wanted nothing more than to carry her to the bedroom, but that nagging feeling he'd had earlier was back. Something was wrong. She kissed him as if it were going to be the last time, and that scared Nate to death.

"I didn't expect to see you tonight," she said when they came up for air. "But I'm really glad you're here."

"There's no other place I'd rather be. Besides, I couldn't let you back out of the special evening I had planned."

Nate placed a kiss on her forehead and then moved to the table where he'd set the bags.

"Something smells delicious," Liberty said as he pulled out several containers and set them on the table. "Wait. You cooked for me? You didn't tell me you were cooking tonight."

"It was supposed to be a surprise."

"Oh, I'm sorry, honey. You mentioned us having dinner, but I didn't know you were going to cook."

"Does it matter?" He grabbed plates and wine glasses from one of the upper cabinets, and then pulled opened the utensils' drawer.

"Yes, it matters. Had I known, I wouldn't have canceled. You shouldn't have gone through so much trouble."

He frowned at her. "Why not?"

"Because." Liberty ran her hand through her disheveled hair nervously. She had let it grow out and now it was past her shoulders.

"Come here." He looped an arm around her waist, pulling her against the side of his body. "Tell me what's going on."

She rested her head against his chest and sighed, her arms tightening around his waist. His worry radar kicked into high gear.

"It's nothing we really have to discuss right now." She pulled out of his hold and placed cloth napkins on the table. If he wasn't so concerned, he'd smiled at the gesture. Occasionally, she did or said things that reminded him of the posh lifestyle she'd lived after graduating. His mother only put out cloth napkins during special occasions whereas Liberty used them whenever they ate at her place.

"I'm worried about you." Nate pulled out a chair for her and then sat in the one on the other side of the two-seater table.

Liberty reached across the table and squeezed his hand. "You worry too much."

Nate lifted her hand and kissed the back of her fingers. "It's my job to worry about you."

Sadness filled her eyes and it was like taking a knife to the chest. He wanted to press her to talk to him, but one of the things he had learned from his father was that women talked when they wanted to.

Instead of pressing for information, he'd wait it out. He had no intention of leaving until she told him what was going on.

Glad the food was still warm, Nate loaded their plates with vegan Bolognese, grilled potato salad and kale greens. Normally he was a meat and potatoes guy, but lately he'd been conforming more to her way of eating, at least when she was around.

Small talk about the meal, the coming snow storm, and how they both looked forward to the Cincinnati Bengals game on Sunday, dominated their conversation while eating. Liberty wasn't as tense as she'd been when he first arrived, but the slump of her shoulders and the lack of spark in her eyes had him on alert. Something had happened today, but he couldn't understand why she wouldn't just tell him.

After clearing the table and washing the dishes, Nate carried their wine glasses to the living room. Once they were settled, he said, "Talk to me." The apartment was so small, the living room couldn't accommodate an actual sofa and they were sitting on a love seat. "Remember when we agreed that we would tell each other everything? Whatever it is, baby, we'll get through it. But if I don't know what's happened, I can't help."

After a long hesitation, she said, "LCA and Jenkins & Sons won the bid for the Unity Tower project."

Nate gasped in surprise. "That's great…isn't it?" Confused at why she wasn't doing a happy dance on top of the table, he didn't say anything else hoping she'd continued. This opportunity was huge for her and she had wanted this even more than he and Nick.

"It's wonderful news, but…"

"But?"

"But," she whispered and then stood, effectively putting space between them when she walked to the other side of the room. Her arms were wrapped around her waist as if protecting herself from something. The tension bouncing off of her was palpable.

Nate stood, but kept his distance. "But what, Liberty? What happened?"

She finally met his gaze. "I um, they…" She shook her head and released a frustrated breath. "I'm no longer on the project."

Nate tilted his head in surprise. "Why not? It's because of you LCA was awarded the project."

"No, it's because of both of us. I couldn't have done that proposal by myself."

She had done most of the work, but he didn't bother arguing with her. There was something else going on here. Something she was holding back.

"What reason did they give for pulling you off the project? With all that you've accomplished for them in this short amount of time, you're an asset. Heck, you guys were just awarded the Unity Tower job. That project is huge. Why the hell would they pull you off of it?"

"Eden said the company frowns on their employees dating LCA's business partners and if I wanted to keep my job I had to…"

Nate stopped pacing and turned to her. The full weight of what she was saying knocked him upside the head. "You had to what?" he asked, already knowing the answer.

"I have to stop seeing you."

Another ultimatum. It was like being back in college again when she had told him that she had gotten married. Her ex had offered her a life that Nate couldn't give her. Like now. Her job had given her a chance to regain her independence. A chance to rebuild her self-esteem. What did he have to give her?

Love.

That's all he had to offer. He couldn't promise her riches. Hell, he couldn't even promise her that her renewed self-esteem wouldn't take a hit if she pledged her life to him. All he could promise her was a lifetime of love. He could promise to cherish her until he took his last breath. But would that be enough for her?

"When I left work today, I kept telling myself that this was just another hurdle. I could deal with it. But once I got home…it feels like another failure. I gave that job my all. That should've been enough for them to see my value."

Nate turned away from her, rubbing his hand over his head. He wanted her to be happy and he knew her job and the independence it gave her made her happy. But the asshole in him wanted to give her an ultimatum of his own.

He faced her, his heart constricting at how depressed she seemed.

"I love you enough to let you go…but I can't," he choked out, emotion invading his chest. "I let you walk away from me before without a fight, but I'm not doing that again. You're a part of me. I don't want to live the rest of my life without you."

Nate moved to stand in front of her and dug the small box from his front pocket. He'd been carrying it around for the past few weeks, trying to determine the best time to present it.

He got down on one knee.

Liberty gasped. Her hands flew to her mouth.

Nape flipped the lid of the box open revealing a two-carat halo diamond engagement ring.

"Liberty, I was too late the last time, but… I love you. I love you more than I ever thought I could possibly love another human being. I know how important your job is, but don't leave me. Marry me. I swear I'll do whatever it takes to—"

"Yes," she cried and fell into him, her arms going around his neck.

Nate stood, lifting her off the floor at first with one arm before wrapping his other around her, the ring still in his hand. Overwhelmed, he had to fight his own tears. The fear of almost losing her had his heart beating triple time.

He set her on her feet and slid the ring onto her finger.

"It's so beautiful," Liberty said in awe, her hand outstretched as she admired the diamond.

"We can get it resized since it seems a little loose."

She shook her head. "I'm never taking it off." She brought her hand to her chest, covering it with the other one. "I had no idea. But there's something you have to know, Nate."

Unease racing through him at the sudden serious turn of her facial expression and tone. "What is it?"

"I chose you. Eden fired me because I wasn't willing to walk away from you. I couldn't."

"Wait. What? You…you quit your job…for me?"

She laughed while wiping her eyes. "No, they *fired* me because of you."

They sat on the love seat while Liberty explained the whole conversation between her and her boss. Her former boss. Nate felt even more confident in his decision to pop the question tonight in light of her revelation. They had professed their love for one another months ago, but they'd done that years ago too. Telling him about the ultimatum LCA had given her, Nate felt as if he had been reliving that day back in college all over again.

Thankfully the outcome was different. Instead of keeping the job she was great at, she'd given it up. For him.

"I don't know what to say. I'm glad you chose me, but I hate you had to give up your job."

"It was the right thing to do. I couldn't walk away from you again. It would have killed me. Nothing, especially a job, is as important as you are to me."

"Aw, baby." He kissed her temple and held on to her, never wanting to let her go. "We're going to fight this. There has to be some law that they've broken. We won't let them get away with this."

Liberty shook her head. "I was still on probation. They could let me go at any time for any reason."

Nate leaned back. "You've been with them almost six months. How long was the probation?"

"Six months. I think Isaac got to them."

Nate gave a humorless laugh. "Come on. He might be the shit in Chicago, but you're telling me that he has the power to get this company to let you go?"

"Isaac has his hands in so much." She glanced down, fiddling with the bottom of her shirt. "I, um, called him when I got home."

"Really?"

She nodded. "I wanted to see if he was responsible for what happened today. And more than anything, I want to be done with him once and for all. If I hadn't called, I would've always wondered if he had gotten to LCA."

"What did he say?"

"He said he had nothing to do with me getting fired, and he's never even heard of the company. He also said he has better things to do than to screw with my life."

Nate shook his head. The guy was such an asshole. "Do you believe him?"

Liberty shrugged. "He's a good liar. I'm not sure what to believe. He sounded sincere, and I haven't heard from or seen him since that networking event."

"So now what?" Nate asked.

"I told him it was time we both moved on with our lives. I tried to keep the conversation civil and even wished him well. He didn't really return the sentiment, but said, have a nice life. Then he hung up."

"Well, we're not going to worry about Isaac."

"You're right. I'll eventually find a job that he can't touch."

Nate rubbed his chin. "Isaac has no power over Jenkins & Sons and never will. As for LCA, it would be interesting to see their reaction to you overseeing the Unity Project on our end."

Liberty smiled. "I can't ask you to—"

Nate's cell phone rang and he glanced at the screen. "This is the detective. Maybe they have something."

"Hello."

"Mr. Moore, this is detective Nugent."

"Hi, what's going on? Did you guys find the person?" Nate put the phone on speaker.

"We think so. Does the name, Trevor Swan, ring a bell?"

"No," both Nate and Liberty said.

"All right, are you two able to come down to the station? I'd like for you to check out a video that we got access to. I'd also like for you to see the guy we picked up. We need to know if either of you recognize him."

"We'll be there shortly."

Twenty minutes later, Nate and Liberty sat in a small room that was the size of a closet without windows. They watched a video of the man smashing in Liberty's car windows. She flinched each time the guy swung the bat. But what ran through Nate's mind is that what if the person had gone after her directly? What if he had attacked her instead of her vehicle?

"Where did the video come from?" Liberty asked.

"One of Mr. Moore's neighbors."

When the video ended, Nate sat back in his seat and folded his arms across his chest. "It's been over a month. Why now? Why hadn't they come forward when it happened?"

"They've been on a thirty-day cruise and recently returned." The detective, who'd been sitting across the table from them stood. "Let's take a walk. My partner is talking with the perp now. He doesn't know we have the video and he hasn't admitted to anything."

They were shown to a room with a one-way mirror. On the other side of the glass, a detective and the man in question were sitting across from each other at a table.

"Wait, I've seen that guy before. He's a friend of Angel's. They were together when I ran into her at my cousin's restaurant." Nate explained the encounter to the detective and they all listened as the detective on the other side of the glass continued questioning the man.

"I'm telling you, I don't know what you're talking about. I think I need a lawyer."

"Why would you need a lawyer if you haven't done anything?" the detective asked calmly, as if they were just two friends hanging out.

"Because…"

"Maybe because you maliciously destroyed someone's vehicle? Take a look at this," the detective said. He played the video on a laptop.

The man's whole demeanor changed. Nate knew they had him, and he placed his arm around Liberty's shoulder.

"What made you take your anger out on a car?"

"Because that guy ruined my life!"

Nate frowned, curious to see what this guy thought he had done.

"What guy?" the detective asked.

"Nate. The woman I loved…she…"

"She what?"

"It took me forever to get her to go out with me and then all she talked about was him! Like he was some damn rockstar. I even sent her flowers and she thought they were from him. Then she goes to see Nate and he upsets her. I tried to tell her that she didn't need him, but he was who she wanted. Apparently, I wasn't good enough for her. She left me and moved out of town."

Nate and Liberty exchanged a look, and she laid her head against his shoulder. Nate had heard some crazy things in his life, but this was way over the top. His brother's words, about Nate's good deeds coming back to bite him in the ass, came to mind. He had always tried to treat women right, but he had no control over their reactions to his kindness.

"That guy ruined my life!" The man pounded his fist on the metal table.

Nate couldn't see the detective's expression since his back was to them, but he didn't move. He didn't seem phased by the guy's outburst.

Nate had heard enough. "Do you need anything else from us?" he asked Nugent.

He shook his head. "No, we have enough to charge this guy. I'll let you know if we need anything else from you."

"That was…enlightening," Liberty said as they walked hand in hand out of the police station. "I knew you were all that," she teased. "But I had no idea the power you had over women."

"Ha, ha, ha. I'm just glad this mess is over. Now we can move on with our lives."

She smiled up at him, her whole face lighting up. "I can't wait to spend the rest of my life with you."

"Me too, baby. I love you so much and I plan to spend the rest of *our* lives showing you."

"I can't wait."

Epilogue

Liberty sat at her computer, putting the last touches on an affidavit before she headed out. It was the last item on her to-do list for the week that she hadn't had a chance to finish the day before.

She smiled as she saved the document. Working at Ben's firm as a law clerk was by far the best job she'd ever had. He had hired her shortly after finding out about the situation at LCA. Nate had also brought her on as a consultant for Jenkins & Sons to manage the Unity Tower project. Showing up at the first meeting to discuss the project with her former boss had been sweet justice, but it was working with the Jenkins family that kept a smile on Liberty's face. Now she was juggling two jobs, and happier than she'd been in a long time.

"I guess I shouldn't be surprised that you're here on a Saturday," Ben said, leaning against the door jamb of her office. "I thought we agreed that you would take weekends off."

"I know, but I really wanted to get this affidavit done by Monday. What are you doing here?"

He shrugged and stepped into the office, sitting in the single chair in front of Liberty's desk. Her space was fairly large and nicely decorated. Most importantly, it was hers.

"I work seven days a week. This place is my second home."

Liberty shook her head and printed out the affidavit. "We need to find you a woman."

Ben laughed. "Not you too. Been there and done that. I'm not looking."

"You might as well give up on that idea, babe."

Liberty glanced at the door, surprised to see Nate there already. He had dropped her off at work before running some errands.

"Every woman in the family has tried setting up Uncle Ben on blind dates," Nate said. "He turns the women down before giving them a chance."

Liberty stood as Nate strolled across the office looking as sexy as usual in a long sleeve Henley, black jeans and a pair of Timberland boots on his feet. Just the sight of him made her giddy inside. And when he looked at her, the way he was now, with so much love in his eyes, she felt like the luckiest woman on earth.

"Hey, baby." He gave her a long, sensual kiss.

"Hey, yourself," Liberty said breathily once he let her up for air. She looked forward to doing everything that kiss promised. They had already tested out the desk's stability when they christened it a few days after she was hired. Since there weren't any other flat surfaces, besides the floor, maybe next they'd try out her desk chair.

Nate kissed her again and grinned as if reading her thoughts. "Have I mentioned lately how much I love you?"

"As a matter of fact, you mention it all the time, and I love you too."

"Alrighty then. I think that's my cue to vacate the room." Ben headed to the door.

"Hold up, Uncle Ben. You might want to stick around."

Liberty lifted a brow. Maybe her and Nate's thoughts weren't lined up because what she had in mind required privacy.

"What's up?" Ben asked.

Nate pulled an envelope from his back pocket and held it out to Liberty.

Anxiety inched through her body, and her heart pounded fast and hard inside her chest.

"Is that what I think it is?"

Nate nodded and handed her the envelope.

"Maybe I should give you two some privacy," Ben said.

"No, Ben. You can stay. Whatever's inside affects all of us."

Liberty stared down at the letter in her hand. The only thing that stood between her accomplishing or failing her number one goal was inside the envelope.

"Open it," Nate encouraged, handing her the letter opener that was laying on her desk.

After a slight hesitation, she ripped the envelope open and pulled the letter out. She quickly skimmed it.

"Oh. My. God. I passed!" she screamed, jumping up and down until she leaped into Nate's arms. "I passed!"

"I knew you could do it." Nate kissed her lips before setting her back on the floor.

Liberty placed her hand on her chest, breathing hard as she read the letter a little slower. She glanced up at Nate feeling as if she was going to burst.

"I just…I just can't believe it. It's official. I'm an attorney."

"Well, let me be the first to congratulate you, Attorney Stewart," Ben said and hugged her.

"Thank you, Ben."

"Now go. Get out of here. Celebrate. Monday, we'll discuss your new position: associate lawyer." He walked out, and Liberty squealed.

"Congratulations, baby. I'm so proud of you." Nate wrapped her in his arms and held her tight.

"Thank you, honey. For everything." She pulled out of his hold and shut down her computer. "When I was a little girl, I dreamed of being a lawyer. Originally, I wanted to be one so that I could make enough money to help my parents. Now, I just want to be the best damn lawyer I can be and help as many people as possible."

"I have no doubt that you're going to be the best. Ready to go? We have some serious celebrating to do." He put his arm around her shoulder and guided her to the door. "So, what should I call you? Attorney Stewart? Counselor? Cutie-Pie Lawyer?"

Liberty laughed. "You can call me anything you want, but I think my favorite name will be Mrs. Nathaniel Jenkins-Moore."

"I like the sound of that, and I can't wait to make you my wife."

"And I can't wait to be your wife."

In less than sixty days they would be married. Nate had wanted to get married right after she took the bar, but Liberty wanted them to have an intimate wedding that only included family and close friends. But considering the size of the Jenkins clan, the plans were turning into a bigger event than either of them considered.

Liberty didn't care. She looked forward to marrying this incredible man who had given her a second chance at love. And she had no doubt that being a part of the Jenkins family would be fun and exciting.

She released a contented sigh as they headed to the elevator hand in hand. All of her dreams had finally come true, and she couldn't wait to see what came next.

*

If you enjoyed this book by Sharon C. Cooper,
consider leaving a review on any online book site, review site or
social media outlet.

Join Sharon's Mailing List

To get sneak peeks of upcoming stories and to hear about giveaways that Sharon is sponsoring, click to join her mailing list.

About the Author

Award-winning and bestselling author, Sharon C. Cooper, is a romance-a-holic - loving anything that involves romance with a happily-ever-after, whether in books, movies, or real life. Sharon writes contemporary romance, as well as romantic suspense and enjoys rainy days, carpet picnics, and peanut butter and jelly sandwiches. She's been nominated for numerous awards and is the recipient of an Emma Award for Romantic Suspense of the Year 2015 (Truth or Consequences), Emma Award - Interracial Romance of the Year 2015 (All You'll Ever Need), and BRAB (book club) Award -Breakout Author of the Year 2014. When Sharon is not writing or working, she's hanging out with her amazing husband, doing volunteer work or reading a good book (a romance of course). To read more about Sharon and her novels, visit www.sharoncooper.net

Connect with Sharon Online:

Website: http://sharoncooper.net
Facebook:
http://www.facebook.com/AuthorSharonCCooper21?ref=hl
Twitter: https://twitter.com/#!/Sharon_Cooper1
Subscribe to her blog:
http://sharonccooper.wordpress.com/
Goodreads:
http://www.goodreads.com/author/show/5823574.Sharon_
C_Cooper
Pinterest: https://www.pinterest.com/sharonccooper/

Other Titles by Sharon C. Cooper:

Jenkins & Sons Construction Series (Contemporary Romance)
Love Under Contract
Proposal for Love

Jenkins Family Series (Contemporary Romance)
Best Woman for the Job (Short Story Prequel)
Still the Best Woman for the Job (book 1)
All You'll Ever Need (book 2)
Tempting the Artist (book 3)
Negotiating for Love (book 4)
Seducing the Boss Lady (book 5)
Love At Last (Holiday Novella)

Reunited Series (Romantic Suspense)
Blue Roses (book 1)
Secret Rendezvous (Prequel to Rendezvous with Danger)
Rendezvous with Danger (book 2)
Truth or Consequences (book 3)
Operation Midnight (book 4)

Stand Alones
Something New ("Edgy" Sweet Romance)
Legal Seduction (Harlequin Kimani – Contemporary Romance)
Sin City Temptation (Harlequin Kimani – Contemporary Romance)
A Dose of Passion (Harlequin Kimani – Contemporary Romance)
Model Attraction (Harlequin Kimani – Contemporary Romance)
A Passionate Kiss (Bennett Triplets Series)